THE COMPANION TALES
VOLUME II

STORIES FROM THE REALM

LISA MANIFOLD

Hello!

Welcome to Volume Two of THE COMPANION TALES! This is the second half of the Realm Companion Stories. In this set, you will see what led Drake to agree to Jharak's request in DRAKE'S DILEMMA,; this Tale takes place at the same time AINE'S TALE is happening. See how Cian became who and what he was in CIAN'S TALE, meet a new character who is drawn into the Realm involuntarily in THE ACCIDENTAL TRAVELER, and then the closing story of the Realm in EILOR'S TALE.

I'm really proud of these stories. While you don't need to read them in order to understand what is going on in the Realm, it gives you a broader idea of the characters, and what is happening. These stories were written around the time I was working on RISE OF THE DRAGON KING, so I had a much better idea of who the characters were, and what their story was.

While this is the end of The Realm series...it's not truly the end. You'll see when you read EILOR'S TALE how this all works.

Thank you for being with me on this journey! The Realm started as a simple trilogy, but it's grown, and it's still not done. I love this series, and all the characters, even my crazybro Cian.

So enjoy, and thank you! As always, I love to hear from you. Sign up for my Newsletter to keep up with all my shenanigans!

Lisa

DRAKE'S DILEMMA

A Realm Companion Story
Tale #5

To all my readers, who loved Drake enough to keep asking about him.

PROLOGUE

From REALMS OF THE GOBLIN KING

*D*rake's easy humor vanished. *"No! I don't want it!"* He glared around the room, and stomped over towards the window, kicking one of the chairs at the table as he did so.

Aine, who had ignored Drake's outburst in favor of the fruit plate in front of her, looked up. "You need to. Someone does. The Realm will go to pieces otherwise." She took a bite of fruit and spoke through her chewing. "I'll help you. I can't rule, but I know the court. I can help you, or whomever it is that goes, to sort things out." She focused on the plate again.

"There," Jharak said. "You have an insider who will help you. There's no one else I can trust, Drake."

At the window, hands clenched on the stone sill, Drake's shoulders tensed. Brennan understood. It was hard to resist their father when he was asking for help. He so rarely did so.

The room fell silent, everyone waiting to see what Drake would say. Brennan walked towards his brother and put a hand on his shoulder. "Brother, you are suited for this. I know you don't want it, but you are. You have been my rock for years. It's time to be your own rock."

He knew Drake didn't want this, but he also knew this was the right thing. He could feel it. Even as he didn't want to lose his best friend, Drake needed to find his place that was his, and his alone. Not as a part of the life of another.

"Leave you to your wife? Hope she doesn't brain you in your sleep?" Drake asked, staring down at the sill. "You won't make it a year, brother."

"Well then I'll have the Goblin Realm all to myself," Iris said from the table. "Not a bad deal."

A moment, and then everyone, even Drake, laughed. Brennan shot a glance of gratitude towards Iris, and he could see that Aine smiled. That was a good sign as well. He hadn't seen a smile from her since he'd met her that wasn't tinged with bitterness or sarcasm.

This was genuine, and it gave him hope for Drake and what he could accomplish.

"All right, all right!" Drake hit the sill. "I'll go. I am making no promises, none at all!" He turned to glare at both Jharak and Brennan. "I will go, and see what kind of mess that family of lunatics has left, and only then will I decide whether I stay."

When neither Jharak nor Brennan responded, he continued, "And that's it! That is the only promise you will get from me. If you're going to yoke me to a throne, then I will determine whether or not it's worth it." His gaze landed on Aine. "And you will help me in whatever I need. I'm not going into that nest of vipers blind!"

She nodded, not even looking up from the fruit. "Of course. I want to see the Realm regain its health. I will be happy to help you."

Drake threw up his hands and stomped towards the door. He jerked it open, saying, "I need to go. I've lost my appetite!" The door slammed behind him as he left.

"Well, that went super well," Iris said.

"He'll come round," Jharak didn't sound concerned as he sat down at the table. "He knows it's the best way for all of us."

CHAPTER 1

*D*rake

I heard my father as I slammed from the room. He sounded so sure, so damned smug. As though there was no doubt that I would do exactly what he wanted.

As I always had.

But I wasn't sure if I wanted to. Could I do this? Can I do what Jharak wanted? I wasn't sure.

Maybe that's what irritated me more than anything else. I've been sure about many things. Most of my life. But I wasn't now.

No matter what others in the Fae Realm said about me, I'd never had any desire to be anything other than what I was. I liked where I was in my life. I like being part of Brennan's court, and my home in the Goblin Realm. There is no need for me to seek out anything better. I had a wonderful life.

The small—okay, not so small—matter of Ailla aside, I had no complaints. With my concerns, relating to my actions, I kept my own counsel. There were mine alone, and nothing that anyone else needed to bother with.

If I could step away and see this from any sort of distance, Jharak's request made sense. He needed someone that he could trust, and who else could he trust more than his own son? Well, the son that he'd raised and knew was a good man. Cian had been his son as well.

I shook my head. Cian had not been his son. Not anymore. I needed to take that sort of thought out of my head. It brought up too many things that were not where I should be going.

I stopped down the corridor, not really seeing where I was heading. With my thoughts in such a muddle, my feet led me wherever they wanted to go. When I looked up again, I was in the practice yard.

There were members of the King's Guards at their daily work, and all heads turned to glance at me as I entered the yard. I nodded to the commander, with a slight jerk of my head.

He smiled, and waved a hand towards a pile of swords along the wall of the yard. My hand reached instinctively to my belt, but my sword was not there. I'd left my scabbard off for the family breakfast. Little had I known the sword might have been a good accessory for what awaited me there, I thought with almost a chuckle.

It had been an ambush. But an ambush that I wasn't able to fight against, and that's where my seething anger came from. That realization struck, and I could feel the heat flood into my face. My lips tightened as I felt my teeth grind together. I took a deep breath, and headed for the pile of practice swords.

"Commander," I said as I picked up a sword and hefted it, feeling its balance. "Would you do me the honor?" I turned around and swung the sword back and forth a few times, getting used to the feel of it.

The commander smiled again, his grin wider than before. "My lord Drake, it would indeed be my honor." He bowed from the waist, and then stood idly swinging his sword.

"Very well." My answer was terse. I didn't feel the need to explain. I didn't have to. I knew the commander well, and as one fighting man to another, I knew he would understand my need to do something, to be physical. It was how men like us took out our anger, and our frustration. Go sweat it out in the practice yard.

"Then ready yourself, my lord," he said. His eyes glinted in the sun, and I could see the prospect of pleasure in his face. More than anyone else here, he could potentially best me. Instinctively, he went into a crouch, his sword at the ready. "Whenever you wish to begin, my lord," he drawled the last word.

I felt, rather than saw, his men stop their own work and draw back towards the walls of the practice yard.

Raising my own sword, I took two steps and went to the fray. My training took over, and I put all thoughts of what had just happened this morning out of my mind with the first clash of metal on metal. My thoughts went to measuring my opponent, looking for the hints of an opening, a weakness.

Which is exactly where I should be.

After I'd put myself through all the paces I could, the commander and I called a halt to our sparring. We were both sweating and disheveled. I could see that most of the other Guards had stopped to watch us. I'd been so mad about the situation I found myself in, I hadn't noticed.

"That was a fine session, my lord," the commander said. "I thank you for it."

I wiped at my forehead with my sleeve. "No, I thank you. I was sorely in need of the work, and I apologize if I have taken you or your men from your regular duties."

I couldn't keep interrupting others for my own selfish needs if I were to be the Ki—I stopped myself.

What in the name of all the gods was I thinking?

J woke abruptly. Someone was screaming—

I looked around, feeling the sweat on my body. I was in my room in the Fae Castle. Not wherever I'd been in my dream. What in the name of the moon and starts had I been dreaming about? And who had been screaming? I rubbed at my eyes, trying to grasp the remnants of whatever the dream had been.

I threw my legs over the side of the bed, rubbing at my face and hair. Lighting the candle on the bedside table, I went in search of the pitcher of water I knew was somewhere.

After my session with the commander of the guards, I'd retreated to my rooms where I took a bath, and ignored everyone in my family. It was childish, and I knew it—but I couldn't get out of my own way at this point. It was rare that I had a bad mood that lasted so long, but when it did, I knew to get away from everyone.

The question was, what was it that was making me feel like a sulky child?

In all the years since Jharak and Nerida had adopted me, I'd never been asked to do anything I didn't care to. They had been amazing parents. Nor had Brennan ever asked more of me than I was willing to do. Not really.

Nerida. I groaned. I couldn't even think about her right now. No sooner had the thought crossed my mind than I found myself focusing on all that had happened in the past —had it only been a fortnight? If that. It seemed much longer since Cian burst into the open to create problems and drama wherever he went. The bastard.

But that brought me back to my mother. She'd been angry with Brennan and me since Cian had shown himself to be alive. That had not changed, and although Jharak remained optimistic, I wasn't so sure. At this moment, I didn't know if I could forgive Nerida, mother or no.

Until yesterday, when Cian and Ailla had burst into the Fae Castle, intending to murder everyone that Cian had formally called family, Nerida refused to believe her lost son was planning any such thing. She'd been furious with Brennan and me, and even Jharak, for seeing Cian as he was. He wasn't a brother or son any longer, but some mad and foul creature, bent on destroying all around him.

I hadn't seen her since Jharak escorted her from the great hall where Cian and Ailla had met their death.

Ailla. There was another sore spot. I sighed, pouring myself a glass of water. I would really prefer some wine, but I knew it would only give me a headache in a moment such as this. Nor would it solve anything.

I allowed myself to see Ailla in my mind's eye once more. The part of me that had loved her—and I had loved some part of her, much as it pained me to admit it—could see how truly magnificent she looked in defense of Cian, if one could forget that it was mad Cian she defended.

But I couldn't forget. I felt a pang then—at what, I wasn't sure. Myself, for believing anything that Ailla had ever said or done in relation to me? Guilt for not being true to Brennan? Brennan had been engaged to the crazy woman at the time. Anger that I'd been fooled? All of the aforementioned emotions?

Probably.

I'd spoken to both Brennan and Iris about Ailla. Two of the more uncomfortable moments of my life.

Oddly, that conversation had been less awkward with Iris. Because she was human as well? Because even as she became more fae, like me, she'd always be human in origin? I didn't know. Because she wasn't the one I'd betrayed? Whatever it was, it was nice to know that my brother's wife was so easy to get along with. No matter how maddening she could be at times. And that she didn't hold anything against me.

Less guilt than dealing with Brennan, too. He held nothing against me, either. That made it worse. I'd thought I'd helped him manage his concerns, but with everything that happened from the moment we met Iris, I'd merely set them aside. In speaking with him, I could see he still carried guilt over Cian, even more so now that he'd been part of his death. I sighed. Damn Cian. Dead, and still leaving messes wherever he'd been.

Then there was the fact that Jharak's request to be more than I'd ever aspired to brought all the doubts, all the mistakes I'd ever made right to the forefront.

I can't do this. I cannot do this.

I finished the water and climbed back into bed. No sense in beating myself up tonight. Plenty of time for that tomorrow. I might as well try and get a little more sleep.

---

*W*hen I woke for the second time, the sun poured into my room, and I felt refreshed. More than I'd expected to, given how angry and restless the prior day left me.

What I really wanted to do was leave the castle right now. Go home to the Goblin Realm, and let Jharak handle this mess created by one of his kings and his crazed eldest son.

I sighed. That wasn't my way. So I got up, and got ready to face the day. And all of the people within it.

Leaving my rooms a short time later, I was glad to see that the corridors were empty. I was in no mood for any more company than I had to have today.

But the empty corridors were odd, given the fact that Jharak had mentioned he'd recently increased the presence of the guards throughout the castle. Something about one of the King's Guards disobeying all orders, and running off with a courtier.

The thought made me grin. In my current state, I was glad to know that I wasn't the only one kicking up a fuss against Jharak.

I was so intent in my own thoughts I nearly stepped on someone else in the corridor.

"I beg your pardon," I said automatically, looking down to see who I might have damaged.

Aine gave me a shove with one hand. "You really should be more alert, my lord," she said quietly.

Did she never raise her voice? I resisted the urge to goad her. It was merely my own foul temper at work. Aine didn't deserve to be on the receiving end of it.

"I generally am. I apologize, my lady. I am distracted this morning," I replied formally.

To my surprise, she grinned. It was unexpected, and Aine looked unguarded for a moment. "I suppose you do. The Dragon Realm is no one's idea of a prize or reward."

"I have to concur with you," I grumbled, formality gone.

"It's not beyond help, either," Aine continued. "It merely requires a strong hand from someone not affected by the way things are, the way they've been for so long."

I started to walk again, and Aine walked next to me. Neither of us spoke. I was thinking about what she'd just said. "What does that mean?" I finally asked.

"It means that the former king was poisonous. But there's nothing to say that a strong new king must be as well."

"I don't want to spend the next hundred years fighting former allies of the madman," I replied.

"I don't think it will take one hundred years," Aine said.

I stopped to look at her. "Is that supposed to make me feel better?"

Aine shrugged, her outburst of humor gone. In its place was the calm woman I'd met in the Dragon Realm. "It's not supposed to do anything other than give you my thoughts on the matter. I don't believe it will take that long. People don't love Eilor. Those that knew Cian thought him dangerous, for the most part. While there may be some still loyal to Eilor—I imagine there are a handful—it will not take you a century to demonstrate to the rest of the Realm that your way is better." She put her hands on her hips and looked me up and down. "That is, if your way is truly better." Without waiting for an answer, she walked forward again.

I stared at her, not sure I'd heard correctly. Did she—I hurried to catch up to her. "Am I to understand you are unsure whether I would be a better choice than Eilor?" I was on the verge of being hugely offended. I might not be Brennan, but I surely wasn't as bad as Eilor! Not even on my worst day!

Aine shrugged as she continued to walk. "I don't know. Are you?"

I started to speak, and then stopped. Was I? Was that

really the crux of the matter? Would I be any better than the power mad king who'd disappeared?

I didn't realize that I'd stopped walking until Aine halted ahead of me and turned to face me with a look of impatience. "Are you coming? Or are you going to stand there all day?"

Still shaken at my thoughts, I started forward, catching up with Aine in a few steps. "Where are you going?" I asked, because to remain silent would allow me to think more than I cared to at the moment.

"The same place you are," she answered. "Unless it's somewhere other than the morning meal."

That meant I wouldn't be able to talk things through with Jharak and Brennan. The various swear words that Iris employed would come in handy right now. I didn't really want to air my concerns in front of a group. Father and Brennan would be more than enough. I sighed at the thought.

But with these thoughts, I didn't really have anything else to say to Aine. We walked along, not speaking. It wasn't entirely comfortable.

When we reached Jharak and Nerida's private dining room, I stepped forward and opened the door for Aine. She glanced at me as she entered, her face unreadable. The sunlight seemed especially bright after the darkness of the corridor, and I squinted to allow my eyes to adjust.

Once I did so, I stifled a groan. Everyone who was someone who would try and talk me into this mad scheme was there. Everyone.

Iris and Brennan sat opposite the door. Both smiled at me. Jharak was to the left, at the head of the table. The far end to the right was occupied by Imara, or Mara as she preferred to be called. Iris' formidable grandmother. I noted that Nerida was nowhere to be found. But I hadn't really expected her to be there. Not after all that had happened with Cian. I felt a pang at her absence. It was hard when I also felt fairly put out with her behavior and words to me as of late.

Then I sighed, and took a seat.

"How are you this morning? A few steps away from ripping our arms off and beating us all?" Iris asked. Her tone had far more cheer than was really necessary, I thought.

"For the time being, you may keep all your limbs," I said.

Everyone around the table burst out laughing. Except Aine, who was seated next to me. But she was smiling.

"Well, that's a step in the right direction," Iris grinned, her smile even wider. How was that possible?

"I would not count on that, your ladyship."

"Oh, knock it off, sad sack! Stop being all stoic, or whatever it is you're going for! Why don't we talk about it and see if we can't help you get over yourself?" Iris rolled her eyes.

"What is there to get over?" I asked, the frustration I felt spilling over. I didn't even care that I was being less than polite. Matters had moved beyond that.

In glancing around, I saw that Mara had raised her eyebrows at either my tone or my words. I responded in kind. Formidable she might be, but I wasn't going to be intimidated by her.

"Why it is you're so against doing something that will make things better?" Iris asked.

I wondered if she was the spokesperson. No one else seemed to mind that she was doing all the talking.

"Do we know that it will make things better?" I asked. There was no way I could keep the scorn or disbelief out of my voice. I felt the disapproval of his brother, but Iris wasn't bothered.

"Can it get worse if we just let it go?" She responded. "I mean, the place is a big mess, right?" Iris turned her attention to Aine.

Aine only nodded. "It will be worse when people figure out he's not coming back. There will be nothing that holds people from doing as they wish. With the mindset prevalent in the Dragon Realm, that's probably not a good idea," Aine finished, looking at me.

No one had to ask who 'he' was.

I sighed. There was no way I was going to prevail in this battle. Absolutely no way. I would be on my way to the Dragon Realm in a number of days.

"All right. Stop. I am going to do this, and I will give it my best efforts. You have my word on that. But I will need help," I added, meeting the eyes of everyone around the table.

The noise rose to an almost uncomfortable level as everyone spoke at once.

CHAPTER 2

*O*ne Month Later

*D*rake

I stood in my chamber, looking at the box that Aine had handed me. I knew what was in it. A bunch of jewelry that she suggested we sell. She hadn't gone through the box thoroughly, but I had.

What I'd found felt like a cold hand reaching from the unmarked grave where the previous owner of the box now resided. The box of jewelry had belonged to Ailla. The daughter of the former Dragon King. In love with Brennan's older brother, Cian. Also known as Kelan. Supposedly dead for hundreds of years and now dead with surety.

Ailla. Try as I might, I couldn't shake the thread that connected me to her. I'd felt sadness mixed with relief when she'd died. There was no other way things could have ended. Not after she helped Cian to kidnap Brennan. It didn't mean I was a monster who turned off my feelings.

I just didn't feel good about them. Until now, life was pretty clear. Either you were with my king, or not. That defined my thoughts and actions. Ailla had smashed all those lines and pulled me into a world of grey.

Which is why her jewelry box bothered me. However, if it were just jewelry, I could manage. But I'd rooted around in the box, and at the bottom, found a false bottom. I lifted it up, and the only thing it held was a letter.

Or what I assumed was a letter. I hadn't been able to bring myself to read it. Which angered me. At myself, and at her. The biggest ring in here was a gift from Cian, so I'd better this letter was from him, too.

I didn't want to know what it said. Not really.

I'd put the letter back into the box under the jewelry, and pretended to ignore it, but every time I was alone in my chambers, I could almost hear the damned thing calling to me.

Once you read something, there's no returning those words. They will always be known. I knew, instinctively, that I wouldn't like what I'd find. The more I'd learned of Ailla, from both Aine and Ailla herself, told me that.

I sighed. At some point, however, I needed to stop be a coward and just read it.

But maybe not yet.

There was a hurried knock on my door, and then just as I called out, "Come in," the door opened.

"I'm sorry to burst in if you're busy, but I want to show you something." she said a little breathlessly. Her arms were full, but I couldn't tell what it was.

"Are you all right?" I asked. "What have you been doing?"

"I ran all the way here," she inhaled deeply, then continued. "I found something," she said. The tone of her voice suggested it wasn't a good thing.

"What? Where?"

Eilor, I'd discovered, had been extraordinarily secretive. It wasn't just a matter of figuring out what he's been up to, we had to figure out where he'd hidden documentation of his plans. If, in fact, there was any documentation. I wasn't sure there would be. Secretive people didn't keep notes.

But Aine was sure that he had. "What am I?" She'd asked during one of our discussion on this matter. "Where my parents? Why didn't he expose me to the court until I was older, and less likely to cause comment? He did something, Drake. He did something to me, or with me — I don't know what!"

She'd been, and continue to be, very frustrated at the lack of knowledge of who she was. One thing she was sure of, however. She told me, over and over again, that Eilor had been very crafty and had a long-term plan in mind.

"What did you find?" I asked her now.

In response, she held up three leather bound books.

"What's in them? Have you read any of them?"

"They go back hundreds of years," Aine said. "The first one talks about the fact that he is to become the king. I only looked at the first few pages."

"Well, maybe you'd better take the time to read them." I replied.

"You don't want to read them?"

I shook my head. "I trust you to tell me what's in them. I find the idea of reading the man's words, seeing what he's actually done, really unpleasant. Which is so foolish," I ground out. "But I can't shake this feeling that there's something truly horrific at work here."

She gazed at me with that inscrutable expression. I knew her well enough now to know that it had a lot of thoughts, rather than no thoughts. It was more that she was giving herself a moment to compose those thoughts.

"I think you're right, Drake," she said. "I don't think I'm going to like what I reading here at all. But if it brings me closer to knowing what he's been up to, what we need to look for, or something about me personally, then I need to read it. I wanted to see if you wanted to read them, but since you are fine with me doing it, I will start this evening."

I felt the hot wash of shame flood my cheeks and neck. I should be the one reading the damned things. That's why Jharak had sent me here. Not only bring some order to the Dragon Realm, but to figure out exactly what Eilor had been doing. I shouldn't dump this off on Aine simply because I didn't want to do it.

I sighed. "Leave them with me," I said. "*I'll* start reading them tonight."

She pulled the books closer to her, almost hugging them to her chest. "No," she said, a shadow crossing her eyes. "I want to read them first."

"Are you sure?" I asked, "because I have no problem doing it, even though I'm sure I won't like it."

She hugged the books tighter. "No, I have a suspicion that this is where I'm going to find the answers I've been seeking. I want to read them first."

I could both respect and understand that.

"All right. I'll admit, I'm glad to leave you to that. But if that's how you feel, why did you offer them to me?"

Aine sighed, and I saw that her grip on the books relaxed a little. "Because this is your Realm, Drake. And I don't think I'm going to like what I find within them. But I would rather know than not."

"I understand. If you need something from me, while you're reading whatever he did, come and see me. Oh, and Aine?"

"Yes?"

"It's not my Realm."

"Not yet." With that, she left the room.

---

*T*he next day, I came upon Aine heading for the kitchens. At least, I think that's where she was headed. She looked dazed, which is something I'd never thought I'd apply to a description of her. I recognize the signs of someone hit with something they weren't expecting.

I attempted to draw her out as to what's she's learned. Her eyes, upon inspection, are red. She's been crying. That makes me even more curious as to what she's found, but I don't press her. She tells me a little.

I was right. It was the damn journals.

We eat, making small talk, and when she leaves, I think she's regained some of the strength it will take to read the journals to the end.

She hadn't discovered anything about herself, but I think it's coming. And it won't be good.

I wonder why she won't just ask the dragons. Surely they know if Eilor's been up to no good in regards to them? But maybe they don't know. I notice she doesn't mention them a lot.

One thing I've learned about Aine—she is a carefully guarded secret shrouded in secrecy, and then wrapped in privacy. She doesn't share until she is ready.

While I'm longing to ask for every detail, I think this was a better thought on my part. Not pressing her allows her to trust me. And the longer I'm here, the more I realize we—I—need her as an ally.

I rubbed my forehead, feeling the headache increasing. The walls of the castle closed in, making it feel nearly impossible to breathe.

The room I was in now was one of the most comfortable rooms, and I'd been through many. It was apparent, from the very beginning, that this was not a room regularly used in the previous royal family. For which I was thankful, because even though they were gone, they seemed to leave an ugly residue that I couldn't shake.

It was a small room, and I had a desk brought in, along with a few chairs, and some shelves. There was a large window behind the desk, and the room sat at the southeast corner of the castle. So I got a lot of light in the room daily. Figures, I thought, that they didn't use this room. Those who worked in the shadows did not care for the sunlight.

And unless I was out seeking information, this is where I spent most of my time. I certainly didn't use the king's chambers. I wasn't sure that I was going to be the king. No need to add to the rumors. There was also the fact that I didn't like the way that they felt. They were too imbued with the presence of their former owner.

Which was a problem in and of itself. I ran my hands through my hair, wondering for the hundredth time, where was Eilor? Since the confrontation at the Fae Castle with my father and brother that had left both Cian and Ailla dead, Eilor had not been seen.

This cursed place. After a month, I still couldn't get the traces out of the people who had lived and ruled here before from it. Echoes of the madness of Cian and Ailla and Eilor were everywhere.

It was in the people who worked in the castle. I had never seen fae such as these before. I didn't want to admit

it, but Aine had been right. These people needed something. I wasn't sure it was me that they needed, but these
people had suffered greatly under Eilor.

I cursed again. How it was the man had kept all of his
horrific projects quiet? I answered my own question before
I'd even finished asking it.

Fear. The people of the Dragon Realm were afraid. In
the case of the servants, cowed. Possibly beaten, although I
hadn't gotten anyone to admit such as of yet. They didn't
trust me.

Which told me they'd probably been beaten within an
inch of their lives. Worse, I'd seen how they reacted to
Aine. I would bet my good sword that it had been done
magically as well as physically. Somehow, she was mixed up
in that, although I didn't think she'd been hurting people.

No, it was more that she inspired fear. There was something about her…when I thought about her, I could understand, and I didn't know much about her. I was not as
trusting as my brother, the Goblin King, or my father, the
Fae King.

I sighed. If the two of them had their way, they'd add
another king to the family. Drake, the Dragon King. I
grimaced at the thought. I didn't want to be a king, and
after a month here, in my potential kingdom, I really didn't
want to be the king of the Dragon Realm.

When Aine, that strange girl who'd grown up here, in
the shadows of whatever it was the mad bastard Eilor, the
former king, was doing, said that there were problems, she
had not been putting it strongly enough.

Problems would have been fine. Problems usually
meant that at some point, they could be managed.

I didn't even know what to call this. A sickness, maybe.
The madness of Eilor, and his daughter, Ailla, and their
pet psycho, as Iris called him, Cían, had left a mark here. It

wasn't obvious, but it went deep. It would take time for this to fade, and I worried that I wouldn't be able to manage it.

The door made a *shush* as it opened, and when I turned around, Aine stood next to me. She held the journals. The look on her face was—it wasn't something I'd seen before. As much as I'd resented being saddled with her, she'd been helpful once we'd arrived here. My feelings weren't really fair, either. I knew that. She was merely part of my anger at being put in a position I didn't want to be in.

At night, when alone, I regularly contemplated on how I could hand this over to Aine and be done with all the various issues of the Dragon Realm.

But Aine had been right. Back at the Fae Castle, she'd said that she couldn't rule. That it would never work. I saw how people shrank from her. It wasn't overt. It was very subtle. But they were afraid of her. I didn't know why; neither did she. But we both saw it.

Eilor, again, probably. The bastard. My vocabulary seemed stuck when it came to the former king.

"Yes?" I asked. After a month, we'd developed a shorthand when speaking. I liked that she didn't feel the need to chatter on. With all the other things wearing on me, it was nice to be around someone who could be quiet.

"I need to talk to you about something," she said. The tone of her voice suggested it wasn't a good thing.

"What?"

"I know what Eilor was doing."

"You've finished the journals?"

"I've gotten through them to the place where they told the story of me."

"And?"

"It's not good." Her lips pressed together.

She looked on the verge of crying. Twice in a week. That wasn't good.

"It's about Eilor. Tell me everything. There's nothing you can't tell me," I added.

Her eyes flew to mine, and I could see the distrust in them. "This is horrid, Drake. There is no other way to describe it."

I shrugged. "I don't think he did anything positive. Not that I've found so far, anyway."

She sighed.

"Sit."

Aine sat down slowly, and then eased back in to the chair. She set the journals on my desk. "This may take a while."

"I have plenty of time."

She took a deep breath, looking at her lap.

This was going to be bad.

CHAPTER 3

*A*ine She took another deep breath. This was the point where she needed to be honest, and tell him the entire truth. She wasn't sure how he'd take it.

But after the dream, and after hearing the voice—Fangorn's voice, she was sure of it—she had to find the entrance to the dragons.

Fangorn had called her "daughter." What did that mean? She knew what she hoped it meant, but…she wasn't sure.

"I am unsure of where to begin."

"The beginning?" His tone was sarcastic, but his expression was kind.

"It's difficult to know where the beginning is. I suppose…" she considered. "I need to go back to before everything happened. I followed Ailla and Cian one day. They went through the wall—don't ask, I'll explain, and then down a long stairway. At the bottom, underneath this castle, there is a large cavern. That's where the dragons are."

Drake sat up straight. "The dragons? Are you finally going to tell me where they are?"

"I'm going to tell you the truth."

"And that is?" His gaze narrowed.

"I don't know where they are—or rather, I don't know how to get to them."

"But—" he held up a hand. "You said, you inferred—"

"Yes. I did." She held his gaze. She had inferred.

He stared back, then a grin spread across his face. "That was strategic, Aine. And I appreciate strategy. It will irritate my father, so there's that. But well done. So please continue with this confession." He leaned back, clasping his hands in front of him with an air of expectation.

"I saw them only once. The one time when I snuck behind Ailla when she went down to their cavern. Afterwards, when they'd come back into the castle, I couldn't find the entrance again. Ailla wasn't supposed to be there. She was clear that Cian could not go on about it."

She leaned back now. The worst was over. "I tried and tried, but I couldn't find the entrance. It was obviously enchanted. Now that I know what Eilor was doing, I know why it was enchanted."

"What else did you read in the journals? What was he doing?"

She tells him. All of it. As she comes to the end of what she's read, her voice trails away. She can't help the shame she feels at being part of this—even though she had nothing to do with it, other than be born into the horrific schemes of Eilor.

"What do you want to do?" He asks.

"I will leave these with you. Please tell Taranath, Jharak, whomever you feel needs to know. I want to find out how to get into the dragons' cavern again. I can do nothing more until I am able to talk to Fangorn." She hopes that is the one she'll talk with. She won't admit to anyone she hasn't found them yet.

"Will you be all right?"

"I wanted the truth, and I have found it. It's horrible, but better than lies. I have a brother, Drake. I will find Fangorn, and then I will find my brother." She can hear the iron in her voice.

Drake sends her away, and she's glad, for once, that someone else is making the decisions. She goes straight to bed.

Once there, she dreams, and in her dreams, Fangorn calls to her. After she sees a boy with a pack on his shoulder.

When she wakes, she is alert as though she was never asleep. Tossing back the bedclothes, she goes to the corridor where Eilor's rooms were.

Drake hasn't moved into them, and after she cleaned them out, no one has gone there with any regularity. She walks slowly, looking from side to side. At a torch that is mounted higher than the rest, she stops. She presses a stone three below the torch.

Nothing happens.

Her shoulders sag with disappointment. She was sure she was on the right track. That's what her feelings told her —but they were wrong.

As she contemplated what to do next, a small door opens as the stones slide to the side.

She's found it. She peers in. This is the stairway. She knows it. The feeling of rightness races through her, like lightning from a storm.

"I'm coming," she says as she steps inside the doorway. When she takes another step, the door closes behind her.

The torch down the stairway lights as if by an unseen hand.

She's found them.

As before, she smelled them before she saw them. Dragons had an underlying sent of sulfur, and it smelled like heat before she reached the bottom of the staircase. Aine stopped, her hand on the wall. The stones were warm. They'd been warm the last time, too. She stepped off of the staircase, and into the large cavern. The area where she stood was an open area, surrounded by ten large cells. There is no other way to call them anything but cells. They were indentations within the cavern, and large metal bars blocked them off from the rest of the cavern.

Torches lit as she walked further into the open area. They were all sleeping, smoke curling in a variety of vertical patterns. Some of the dragons had their heads close to the bars. Others, all she could see was the tail. Or the back end. Her eyes moved across the various cages, counting, making sure they were all there. When she got to the seventh cage she gasped.

The dragon—for she'd seen a dragon in every cage when she'd been here prior—was missing. There was no dragon in the cage. They were all too big to be hiding.

How could that be? She would've heard — everyone would've heard — had a dragon escaped. They were not small. There was no way out. She had no idea how they'd even been brought here.

She got to the bars of the cage with the missing dragon, and clutched them. She peered in, hoping against hope to see — what was that? There was something — someone — at the back of the cage.

"Hello?" She spoke softly.

Someone — it looked to be a man, walked from the back of the cage towards the front. As he approached, she took a few steps back. He was tall, with hair that looked almost... Blue. It was such a dark black, it had a inky look as the light from the torches caught it. He was... naked. As he got closer, she saw that his eyes were large, almost unnaturally green. The pupils looked more vertical than rounded.

"Who are you?" His voice seemed even bigger than he was, rumbling through the cavern.

"Who are you?" she asked, unnerved by the timbre of his voice.

"I am Fangorn. If there is a task you wish of me, you will need to clothe me." His voice rumbled through her very bones.

"Why would I wish you to complete a task?" She asked.

"Is that not why you have woken me?" Fangorn asked.

"I didn't wake you at all," she said. "All I have done is walked down to the cavern."

He looked perplexed. "Have you been here before?"

She nodded. "Once. I've been looking for you. I wanted to see if all of the dragons were all right."

His entire face changed. It actually seems to look more blue, and he looked angry. "All right?" He asked slowly. "How can I, or my brethren, be all right? We're trapped here, in cages, like what we are mere rabbits to be kept for food."

"You are not one of the dragons that was part of the great war?" She asked. She had heard from Eilor that the dragons were kept here so they could not rise again. So they could not wreak havoc upon the Realms, or at least, not until Eilor was ready to let them.

"Of course I am one of those dragons," Fangorn said. "That does not make the captivity any less than what it is, or any better."

"Would you rather die?" She asked.

He stepped forward, and she was struck by the overwhelming physical presence of him. While his claim to be a dragon, standing there as a naked man, sounded silly she believed every word of it. He radiated power. The fact that he was naked took nothing away from it.

"I would rather be dead than to live like this. This is not living, girl. Who are you?" He sounded angrier, and his voice deepened, if that was even possible.

"My name is Aine." She was so surprised, she answered his question without thinking. It was the effect of his voice, she thought.

He moved to the bars of the cage, gripping them so tightly. She could see the whites of his knuckles. "Aine? You said your name is… Aine?" He spoke as though he knew her. It scared her.

"Yes, why? I've never met you before."

"Where is your mother?" The question cracked like a whip.

"I… I don't know. I don't know are either of my parents are. Eilor never told me…?" Her voice trailed away as his eyes begin to gleam. "Are you the Fangorn described in the journals?"

Something that she asked struck him. He removed his hands, the bars, apparently noticing that he was frightening her. When he spoke again, while still deep, his voice seemed softer. "Why do you ask about the journals?"

"Because I've read them, and I've read the… things…Eilor did."

"Where's Eilor?" He asked and she could hear the hatred in his voice when he said the name Eilor.

"I don't know. He's disappeared. His daughter, and… It doesn't matter. Essentially, all the people who knew about the dragons are gone."

"So what brings you here?"

"I followed Ailla down here one day. I've tried to get back ever since. I find the dragons… calming."

He crossed his arms, studying her. She could swear that he looked almost ready to smile. But she didn't want to make that assumption. He got a dragon out of here somehow. She wasn't sure that the bars would keep her safe from him.

"So you know nothing of your parents?"

She shook her head. "No, I don't. Well, I didn't. Now I do, and it…it breaks my heart. Did you know them?"

"What did you read in the journals?"

"You know about those?"

"I do. He's kept them a long time."

She stepped forward, eagerly. "What else can you tell me?"

It was amazing, watching his face. It shuttered as clearly as someone closing up the windows of a house. "If you want the truth, I would guess he put it there rather than anywhere else"

"What I read was the truth?" Her voice dropped. What she'd read had been horrible.

"Yes. However bad it sounds, it was worse."

"Oh, no." Her voice came out in a creaky whisper.

"What do you want from me?"

"I want to help you."

"Do you know who you are to me?"

"You are Fangorn, and Lionel, my father was your son."

"Yes, daughter."

It was the voice she'd heard in her dream. "It was you," she breathed. "You helped me find it. Why now?"

"You were ready."

She stared at him for a long time. "You are my grand-father," she said.

He nodded regally. "I am, and I am pleased to meet you. I am sorry that it has to be like this."

"You can shift when you want to?" Eilor's journals made it seem like he couldn't shift without Eilor anymore.

A light shone from the cage that was so bright, she had to cover her eyes. As quickly as it appeared, it was gone. When she looked back at the cage, Fangorn was gone, and the blue dragon sat in the cage, looking at her with gleaming green eyes.

"Are all of you this way?"

He shook his head. "No. I alone can change my form. All of us can speak, when we are awake, and should we choose to. Most of us have taken a vow of silence, as the only person who wished to speak with us was Eilor." The name came out as a growl.

"I thought he was selected as the guardian of you."

He slashed a paw that had long claws in her direction. "A sorrier steward I've never met. He woke us, which I was led to believe would not happen, and immediately began seeing how he could put us to use. He made sure to rein-force these," The claws gestured at the cavern cave, "Because we would have killed him otherwise. As he well knew."

"How is it you are a shifter?"

He sighed, a puff of sulfur-tinted air ruffling her hair. "I have both Fae and dragon in my lineage. Many years ago, the two races were not as far apart as one might think. The result is that I can shift between forms."

"Why don't you escape?"

"I cannot pass the bars. Only Eilor may open them, and I am bound to his command. He is not dead," Fangorn finished.

"How can you tell?" She asked.

"Because I could—we could—be free," he said simply.

"I will help you," she said.

"Not until Eilor is dead," he replied. Then he turned away and moved into the shadows of the cage.

The conversation was over.

Aine stood for another moment, but it was clear that Fangorn had nothing further to say. She turned and climbed the stairs, trying to process all that she'd heard.

Once she'd reached the top of the staircase, she hurried into her room. She needed to decide what to do next.

———

O ver the next week, she visited the caverns every day. She and Fangorn talked about everything, and he roared at her when she told him that she had found Jharak, the Fae King, likable.

Finally, after a long silence where they both stared at the walls, he said, "I should like to meet the son of Jharak who is here."

She is so shocked at his request she stares at him for a moment, unsure of what to say.

"When?" She finally managed.

"I will leave that to you. I know you haven't told him that we are meeting. You will need to let him know the truth, and then you may bring him down here. But you must understand, I will allow no harm to come to my brethren."

"Nor will I," she said.

As in her dream, his claw came out from the bars, and she stepped toward it. He curled two of his longest claws into her hair. Rather than worrying that a ferocious creature had his claws tangled in her hair, she felt the warm acceptance of family. She closed her eyes, enjoying the closeness.

"I know," he said. "We will keep them safe."

She couldn't remember when she'd felt so content.

CHAPTER 4

*D*rake

I sought out Aine at breakfast over the next week. She was distracted. I didn't inquire too deeply. She would tell me in her own time.

Besides, I was dealing with a rash of magical wards throughout the castle. I thanked the sun and stars that Brennan continued to allow his mage, Taranath, to be here. We'd spent the last three days searching them out and breaking the wards.

She came into my study one afternoon, sitting down without asking if she was interrupting. "You've done well with the wards, Drake. I didn't know he'd done that."

I shrugged. "It's rather his standard, isn't it? To make things as negative and problematic as possible?"

She laughed, a low chuckle that I was pleased to hear. "That was his manner of operating. He was never open or honest, so he assumed that everyone else was the same way."

"Well, I shall keep that in mind. Taranath and I are

nearly done with the areas of the castle where people are moving around frequently."

"You're doing well," she said again.

"I have a feeling removing the influence of Eilor will be a long-term affair. Now that we've sorted the latest in the mad bastard's crazy scheming, do you have some time to go over a few things with me?"

She took a chair across from me. "How can I help you? Have you begun reading them yet?"

I knew she was talking about the journals. I'd locked them away and hadn't looked at them. "No. I've had more immediate problems."

Aine smiled. Her demeanor was so calm, she rarely raised her voice or showed a great deal of inflection. But I was learning that even the smallest change in the way that she spoke said a great deal about how she felt.

"I've made a list," I handed her a piece of parchment with names written down it, "of all the people that seem like they have a chance to be normal again. I have a second list," I took another piece of parchment and handed it across to her, "of people that I think will be a problem no matter what. I would like to know your thoughts on all of these people."

She held the two pieces of parchment in her hands. Her eyes we steady on me as she looked over the tops of the lists. "You wish for me to spy on the people of my own court?"

"Are they really your court? That wasn't the impression that I got when you spoke of the Dragon Court," I said quickly.

Her lips thinned, ever so slightly, and I knew that I'd scored a point with her. One of the reasons that she had claimed she could not effectively rule was that the people of the court did not trust her.

I knew I probably wasn't being fair, but this was information I needed to know. I needed to know who I could trust and who would bear watching. Thankfully, the list of those that I felt had the capacity for some trustworthiness was longer than the list of those I suspected were going to be problematic.

At least I felt I could trust Aine. I didn't know much about her, which drove me a bit mad, but I also didn't feel like she lied to me.

She kept secrets. That much I knew. Again, however, I didn't think she was keeping them so that she could harm me or my family. That was the difference—secrets were fine that didn't harm others. Like, when would she lead us to the dragons?

It was a good thing I was patient when it came to gathering information. As much as I wasn't sure of her, she was not sure of me. Given how she'd grown up—Eilor was the only father figure she'd ever known, and that cannot have been positive—her lack of trust was understandable.

I could also be patient because I felt like the trust between us would come.

I waited in silence as Aine looked over the two lists. I'd been keeping these pretty much since I came here, adding, subtracting, and moving around the people on the list as he spent more time in the Dragon Court.

If I agreed to do this, it wouldn't be easy.

She finally looked up. "I think you've done a good job here, but if you lend me your pen, I'll make a few corrections."

Wordlessly, I handed over the quill, and watched as she made a few scratches on both sheets.

She handed them back to me, and I looked over her corrections. "Really, this?" I turned the sheet around with the list of trustworthy people on it, pointing to where she scratched off the name of a woman and her son. "You don't think they're trustworthy?"

She shook her head. "No, that woman was very close with Ailla, and I got the impression they spoke quite a bit to one another. She may know more than you'd be comfortable with."

"You would know better than me," I said, putting the name of the woman and her son onto the list of those to be watched. "That's why you're here, and I'm glad for it."

"Are you?" she asked quietly.

Not taking my eyes from the lists, I nodded. "Yes. I'm no good at this sort of thing. If there someone who needs to be dealt with, a task that needs doing, or some sort of fighting, I'm your man. But dealing with people? Working around all the social constraints? Figuring out the motivations of the people around me? I'm no good at that."

"Well, you did a good job with your two lists," Aine said with a smile.

"Yes, and it took me over a month," I said dryly, finally looking up at her. "Not the best thing, when you have to make decisions as a leader."

"Like anything else, that can be learned," she replied.

I tossed the paper in front of me onto the desk in a flare of frustration. Leaning back in the chair, clasping my hands behind my head, I tried to ease the knot in my shoulders. "Yes, anything can be learned! But at what cost? And how long does it take? And if I take too long, since we are speaking of me here, how much harm can be done in the meantime?"

Unable to sit still with the strength of my thoughts, I got up and began pacing behind the chair, in front of the window. This castle radiated darkness and gloom. It felt good to stand in sunlight. "Father needs to know that this kingdom is secure! I can't back out of this! I can't tell him much of anything right now! I've never been so frustrated in my life! Fighting is easy, but this!" I threw up my hands. "This, this is... this is... just crazy! Not to mention that there are explosions lurking, waiting to hurt the people here!"

Aine watched this with no expression on her face. "Should I tell you what I'm hearing throughout the court about you?"

I stopped my pacing and gripped the chair in front of him as he stared at her. "Really, Aine? You have to ask? If you have information of how the court feels about this possible move of my father's, you need to let me know!"

"People have been slow to trust me," she said, showing no offense at my tone. "It's taken a little while for them to open up."

"Well? What do they say?"

*A*ine
She watched him, so tense, gripping the back of the chair as if he were holding on in order to survive. This was a different Drake than she'd seen at his father's court. He'd been angry, and sarcastic, and his wit had been biting. Of course, she'd only seen him when he was in the middle of rescuing his brother, or under duress to do as his father asked, so perhaps it wasn't a fair comparison.

Here, he seemed out of place. She felt for him. She often felt out of place, and she understood his frustration. He wasn't used to being the outsider. The one who was not trusted. Here, conversations stopped when he came near.

She didn't fare much better. Eilor had allowed an air of mystery and suspicion to grow around her. It suited his purposes to have the court keep their distance from her.

She knew that she'd found part of the answer in the journals. People knew that Eilor was involved in some sort of plotting. What, no one knew. After reading the journals, she knew that no one could have guessed the depth of his plans. But they knew he was up to something, and it didn't feel good to them.

She knew it with even greater surety when she'd seen the sleeping dragons. Only she knew where they were, and she only knew that because she'd followed Ailla and Cían down to the caverns where they were kept one day one year prior. Had they known she was there, she would have been killed. From what Ailla had said at the time, she wasn't even supposed to be there. Aine knew that she would fare worse than the daughter of the king if discovered.

Try as she had, she had not been able to find the door again. She couldn't even remember exactly where she'd been in the castle when she followed them in. Which meant there had to be a spell on it. Figures. Ailla was like that. Always hiding things, always hiding what she was doing.

There was no mention in the court of the dragons below the castle. No mention of them in any fashion. Wouldn't the fate and care of eleven large dragons be of some interest? Everyone spoke of the dragons as though they were long gone.

Based on all of that, even before the journals, she knew then that Eilor was up to something.

All she knew was that when she'd seen the first dragon, large, sleeping, slight puffs of wispy smoke issuing from his nostrils as he breathed, she could feel his heartbeat. She could feel his strength, his power—and it resonated within her.

That was not the sort of thing you spoke about in casual conversation.

Aine had wished for more knowledge—a hint, a clue—something—and in spite of paying attention to everything but Ailla and Cian, she'd learned nothing.

But when she remembered the dragons, she had a sense of being complete and of such longing that she thought she might cry.

So the journals were the best source of information right now. Whether it would be for her good or ill, she didn't know. She was glad that she'd offered Drake the chance to read them, and equally glad he'd said no initially. That allowed her the time to process them. It was something to consider that when she and Taranath had found them, she wouldn't let him read them. And now, Drake had them.

But it wouldn't surprise her. Or take her off guard.

Something to consider later. Not now.

To the matter at hand, she could identify with Drake's feeling out of place, and out of step.

People weren't sure what to make of him. He was the son of the Fae King, and originally a human. Aine found that aspect of him fascinating. He looked no different from any of the fae she saw daily, but maybe she missed something other fae did not.

Eilor had quietly sown distrust of Jharak, without coming out and saying a thing. The court as a whole had been surprised when he'd allowed Ailla to become betrothed to Brennan. Aine had always assumed there was something in it for him.

Now she knew, even though the rest of the court would never hear of it. It had been part of the plan to overthrow both the other fae kings, and take over all of the realms. Aine rather thought that Cian and Ailla had sent those plans down a path that Eilor had not wanted—but again, she wasn't sure.

Almost sure, however. if there had been any other reason, she felt certain that he would have made an appearance, apologizing for his daughter, and excusing the fact that he'd hidden the king's son away for hundreds of years.

But he hadn't. To her, that only meant one thing. He was on the run, and in hiding. She didn't think anyone would find him until he wanted to be found. She knew that Jharak, Brennan and Drake all thought he'd died—but she knew better.

He was too crafty to give up by dying. And she knew he'd worked for a long time for—whatever it was he'd been planning to come to fruition.

No, he was still alive. She felt certain they'd learn it at the worst possible time.

This was not the place to focus on that. She had to help Drake find his place—and part of that would be letting him know where he stood with the court.

"They are not sure if you are here to help, or only find those loyal to Eilor and Ailla. I'll tell you that no one seems to have realized that Cían and Kelan were the same people. The scar kind of threw them—everyone mentions it. Those who had seen Cían before he was removed from the Fae Castle are a small group."

"Most fae, were they hurt as Cian had been, would have had the scar healed."

She nodded. "Yes, that's what people mention. That he must have been even odder than suspected, because who wants a scar? Even back then, when Cian was hurt, Eilor didn't encourage a lot of visiting to other courts. He preferred his court isolated, dependent on him. In short, they're scared. They're not sure what your end game is.

And if you're part of this court, in your mind, everyone has an end game." She threaded her fingers together in front of her.

Drake sighed. "I wish they would believe me——"

She held up a hand. "They can't, Drake. You need to understand that. They cannot. Nothing was free, nothing was simple, and everything had strings and repercussions here."

He stared at her for a moment, not speaking. Finally, he said, "What a horrible way to live."

"It's not really living at all. I wouldn't have wished my position on many, as I wasn't allowed to socialize with others much, and my constant companion was Ailla, and then Cían if I was lucky," she grimaced, "but I had it easier. I always knew my place. Ailla always hated me, and Cían…Cían treated me oddly."

"What do you mean?"

She could tell he was interested. "I think that Cían had an overdone idea of himself, and who he was. What he had to offer. But he knew that I was important to Eilor, and that made me of interest to him." She laughed a little. "Although it seemed to be a matter of distress that he was interested in a little nobody like me. It hurt his pride."

Drake laughed. "In spite of denigrating him, he had two very strong women who loved him. He must have done something to inspire that depth of feeling. I don't know what it was—did Ailla enjoy crazed people? Did Dhysara? Because there was something—you saw them. They were both devoted."

"Dhysara isn't crazy."

"I disagree, Aine." Drake leaned forward in his chair. "She was raised here. With Eilor as her main father figure. You didn't hear her when Taranath and Iris and I visited her before we found the castle where you were. She believed that much had been stolen from her, that Jharak and particularly Brennan were to blame. She was a child when her father died. Who fed her these notions? Who encouraged this manner of thought?"

She considered his words before speaking. He had a point. Drake might rant on that he was a warrior, and a fighter, not a scholar—but he was observant, with a quick, keen mind. She liked that about him. He spoke his mind almost immediately, with no sense of manipulation, or thought of how it might benefit him. He was an honorable man. It made her realize how none of the men she knew were anything like him. In any way.

That wasn't entirely true. It was true in the past, but not now. The men she knew, the men she would allow herself to trust, they were not like Eilor and Cían. Jharak was a good man. Brennan was a good man. And Drake was a good man.

"Well, obviously Eilor. He had everyone fooled. Everyone except the few people around him that knew who he really was, what he really wanted." At first, she thought Eilor was her father. After a time, particularly after she'd seen him with Ailla, she knew he wasn't. She knew that she meant nothing to him, nothing other than a realization of his plans.

"Then not many people knew that he was going to attempt to take over all the Realms?" Drake asked.

Aine shook her head. "I think that people started to realize, after a while, that he was not a good man. There was definitely something not nice about him. But nothing could be proved. No one had any real facts. He was very clever."

"They're still afraid of him," Drake said, tapping his lists. "People are afraid to talk to me too much, for fear that

Eilor might hear. They don't say that, but I know when people are scared."

"They are scared. If you disagreed too much, you disappeared." She stood. "I'll be in my rooms should you need me."

He smiled at her, and she thought for a moment that he was actually handsome. Then she struck that thought from her mind, because such a thing could never be.

"All right. Let me know should you come across any more wards."

"I will."

On her way back to her rooms, she passed several members of the court in the corridors. They darted their eyes at her, and gave a quick bob, an approximation of a bow, is as they hurried on. It was obvious that they weren't sure where to place her in the hierarchy of the court.

To each, she gave a brief smile. She could manage much more. She knew that Drake found this castle oppressive. She agreed with him. It was. But it was the seat of the Dragon Court. There was really no other castle within the Realm that would hold all the people that needed to be here.

If Drake was to be the king, he would need to find a way to make this castle his own. After Eilor had lived here so long, she wasn't sure what it would take.

When she reached her rooms, she entered and shut the door behind her gratefully. All her life, she thought that what she wanted was to be around people. But now that she was, she found it extremely wearing. They made her tired. And in court, people chattered like the birds.

Lying on the bed, she realized she hadn't seen the dragons in some time. Seeing them always refreshed her. Fangorn had begun to open up, to not treat her as a possible enemy.

She didn't want to let that get away from her. Not for Drake, or anyone else. This was something that was hers.

Which meant she'd need to tell Drake that she'd found the dragons soon. Sooner rather than later. Waiting too long would make him upset, and understandably so.

But she still wanted to keep Fangorn for herself.

Just for a little while.

CHAPTER 5

$\mathcal{D}$rake

I stood, pushing all the paperwork and things away from me. I was tired of all the administrative things that needed to be done to keep the castle running. It had taken me nearly two weeks to sort what was needed. The castle was running out of food, and no one seemed to have the authority to make sure that everyone in the castle got fed.

This is what made Eilor mad, I thought sarcastically. On top of everything else going on. Dragons, who knew where? Wards set to kill people, although I thought we'd managed to negate that as a threat. People skulking about worried they would be in trouble, hurt, killed.

My list of woes were interrupted as the door burst open. Aine came in, and for the first time since I'd met her, she looked flustered. Almost as though she'd run here.

"What's wrong?" I asked.

She put her hand to her chest. "Drake, are you still thinking about whether or not you will accept the throne?"

"I hadn't thought about it since we talked about it last," I said, surprised. Her hand felt…warm.

"You have to," she said, breathing heavily. "You have to."

"What is going on? Why has your opinion changed so strongly?" I could tell that something had upset her.

She held up a hand. "Do you trust me, even a small amount, Drake?"

I frowned. This wasn't going where I thought it would. "I do. I don't know you well, and that is a concern. But you seem to hate what Eilor and his family did even more than I do, so until I know better, that is worth trust. The enemy of my enemy is my friend, and I am willing to call you friend until you show me otherwise."

Normally, I wouldn't have said such a mouthful, but something about her told me that I needed to be honest, and not dissemble or hedge in any fashion.

She nodded, looking down. She was obviously caught in her thoughts. "Then I must ask you to stretch your trust. I cannot tell you what I know, or how I know it—not yet. I have more to learn, and more…" she hesitated, "People to question, but you must trust me—you must take the throne."

"Why?" I asked simply. There was more at work here, and her hesitation made me think that something deeper—read magical—was afoot. That made me nervous, in spite of the fact he said he trusted her. Magic, in this kingdom—it had not served anyone well.

"Because in order for things to become right, to heal, there needs to be another king. There needs to be a good man on the throne. Things in this Realm are tied to the King."

I rolled my eyes in disgust. "Let me guess. Eilor's doing." I wanted to ask details, but I'd just agreed not to.

She nodded, her lips pressed together. "Not only Eilor...but it is the way...the way things are."

"If he is not dead, I will run him through the first instant I see him, should I ever see him again," I grumbled, thinking of all the work, all the mess that Eilor had left behind. It was never-ending, which made me more irritated than anything else.

"You will need to get in line," Aine said.

The tone of her voice made him look at her. A fire that he'd never seen on her burned in her eyes. She was furious.

"Really? What have you learned?" She'd told me about the journals, but...what else had she learned? And how?

"More than I wanted to."

"Well? What is it?"

Aine shook her head. "I can't tell you yet. I need some more time to sort this out."

I clenched my jaw, considering. This wasn't what he wanted to hear. But Jharak and Brennan, and even Iris trusted Aine. So did he, to a point. She was pushing it, withholding information like this.

"I don't like that you're not telling me what you've learned."

"It's not complete," she said, and the fire went down. "I have learned some...what would Iris call it? 'Serious shit'? But I don't have all the information. I want to be able to give you all that you need."

"Need for what?" This back and forth made me exasperated. She spoke in circles, and there were few things I disliked more.

"So we can undo all that he's done. I won't be able to help you if I don't know everything. I will, though."

"How can you be sure of this?" I wanted to trust her, but trusting her also meant that I would be saying yes to the one thing I'd avoided my entire life.

"I have never been more sure of anything in my entire life." The way she said that, in the calm, unruffled manner I associated with her—told me that as far as she was concerned, she was being honest with me, and concealing nothing that she felt I needed to know.

"If I agree to this, I am tying myself to this kingdom," I sighed. "This is not where I wanted to be, Aine. I liked my life before."

Aine stepped close to me, taking my hands in her own. The act of her touching me voluntarily sent a thrill through me; I hadn't expected that. She looked up at me, and I was struck by the dark eyes with the glints of green in them.

How had I not noticed them before? They were striking, and in that moment, I saw—really saw—how striking *she* was.

"Perhaps your time in the Goblin Kingdom, helping your brother, was preparation for this. I don't know you well, Drake, but I think you are meant for more."

"You're just saying that," I pulled my hands away, and walked to the window. It beckoned to me. It spoke of freedom, freedom from the mundane tasks I was drowning in, from being the place where all responsibility landed, from all the petty things I'd begun to hear from the Court— freedom to do as I pleased.

"No, I am not."

"I will never be free again," I said quietly, my gaze locked on the mountains beyond the castle. I could practically hear them.

"No one is free. Everyone is tied to something. Even me, with no family, no apparent ties—I cannot leave here. I couldn't leave the dragons. I couldn't leave these people to suffer more than they have."

"Have you heard them?" I turned around, one hand

clawing through my hair thinking on the parade of courtiers that had found their way to my room over the past day alone. "Have you heard the petty complaints, the anger, the jealousies—it's maddening!"

"They have nothing more, Drake. This is all they were able to do. They had no freedom under Eilor. No one did. But if you can show them that there is another way to live, you can turn the sickness of this Court away, and make it strong and healthy again. You were meant to do this, Drake."

How could she be so calm? "What are you talking about?"

"Your name is Drake. That's another word for dragon. You were named for the dragons from the time you were born."

All right, I didn't like her calm manner of speaking anymore. It sounded like a seer, one of the Aumahnee seers of old, spouting out prophesies that no one ever understood. It made him uncomfortable. I wasn't a prophecy, my life wasn't one, either.

"I was meant to do as I please," I began.

Aine's eyes flared again. "No one is meant to do as they please!" she snapped. "We are all obligated to one thing or another! That's how we get along without beating one another to death. The people who feel no obligations, who are dedicated to themselves only—those are the uncivilized. I don't understand why you're being such a child. You are the son of a king. This is part of being the son of a king."

"No one ever expected me to be a king of anything. I'm human-born."

"And? I have no idea what my lineage is. Yet here I am, advising the future king, and the friend and advisor to other kings. I know that whatever I am, it will come from some horrible plan, some terrible secret that Eilor kept. I am not my past, I am not only my birth." She stepped closer to him. "Neither are you."

"Go away, Aine," I said, my voice low and angry. "I accept that you cannot, or rather will not, tell me everything you have learned. I will allow for you to tell me when you feel you have gathered the information. But I will not be lectured by you on my responsibilities. I know them well."

"Do you?" She asked from right behind me. "Are you sure?"

I didn't turn around. I definitely didn't want to talk to her anymore. I could feel the walls closing in on me, and there was nothing I could do to stop them. I would be stuck in this miserable castle until I died. I let my head fall as I heard the door close behind Aine.

I had the unhappy suspicion I'd just alienated the only friend and ally I had in this place.

I stayed in either my study, or the room I slept in for the next two days, avoiding people, and generally sulking. I knew I was sulking, which made me angrier. But I couldn't seem to shake the black mood that had settled over me.

Worse, Aine had not come back to speak to me about anything. I hadn't seen or heard from her since she left the study.

After you told her to go, my inner voice reminded me. I found that I missed speaking with her, missed her quiet contemplation and view of anything I put before her.

Except when it was something important to her. Then, I dismissed it, and told her to go away. She had always been honest with me and my family. She answered questions as best she could, with the available knowledge she had. If she felt there was reason to delay sharing it, there must have been good reason.

But what she asked of me!

It was no worse than what my father asked. And Aine actually had presented a better reason, one that I understood. I'd seen the sickness in this kingdom. It needed to heal. She said that a new king needed to take the throne to make that happen. She knew more of the depths of the sickness than I did—and she felt I could heal it.

I sighed. It was time to stop hiding.

I wasn't sure what he was going to do. I knew, though, that what I'd been doing, how I'd been behaving, was not how I lived life. I'd behaved as a coward. I'd never faced something I didn't really want to, truthfully. Brennan had always taken that on. Brennan managed it so well, it looked nearly effortless.

Brennan. Why hadn't I thought of that before?

I sighed again. I already knew the answer. Because I didn't want to hear what I was doing wrong. I took the mirror from my pouch.

"Brother," I said. It took a moment, but Brennan appeared.

"Drake! How are you? I've been concerned. We've not heard from you in a number of days."

I sat down on of the old-fashioned chairs that inhabited my sleeping quarters. "I have not had much that is positive to share. Aine was correct. This Realm is suffering. The people are unhappy, and scared. Eilor was up to something—I don't know what," I said, holding up a hand to forestall any questions, "But Aine is seeking answers. She has not found all of them as of yet, but I am trusting that she will let us know when she does."

"What is the overall state of the Realm? The Court?"

"Poor, Brennan. The people are frightened but no one will speak of exactly why. They are not sure whether to trust me. Eilor did not work to make sure that his Realm had what it needed. From looking at the records in the Treasury, which only he kept, from what I can tell, he spent a great deal of the Realm's resources on unnamed items. I don't know what they are. He had a system of note taking that I have yet to decipher."

"So he was a terrible king, and steward. He and Ailla always looked so well-off," Brennan mused.

"It was an act. Actually, if I am reading it right, the Realm should be well off. There are resources to be traded from here. But it looks as though Eilor kept them for his own uses, of which I am not sure of." I couldn't help myself – I burst out with a groan of frustration.

"And the complaints! You should be thrilled that the goblins can't complain like this! I have a small room I am using as a study, and now that people have learned where I am, they come in at all hours, all wanting to let me know about something I am to fix for them! I don't know how to fix it! I barely have an understanding of all that is wrong! Except that it's all wrong!" I could hear my voice rising as I spoke but I didn't stop. It felt good to just get this out, to be heard. I opened my mouth to continue, and realized this was why the people of the court were finding their way to me.

They needed to let someone know their frustrations. They needed to know that someone had heard them, that there was a chance their concerns would be addressed. All this time, I felt untrusted, and an outsider—but in reality, they were showing me, in perhaps the only way they knew —that I was becoming something more.

"Drake? Are you all right?"

Oh. I'd stopped, getting lost in my thoughts, and had ceased speaking. Great. One more thing for Brennan to needle me over. "I am. I just had a realization, and—"

"Oh, good. It's about time one of those occurred for you," Brennan said dryly. "I was beginning to wonder."

"Shut it, know it all," I smiled, and it felt like the first real smile I'd cracked in days.

"Are your problems all solved now, lordship?" Brennan asked in the same tone I used when I called him 'lordship'. "Can I get back to my own concerns? I've got my own Realm to manage. And a pregnant wife. You, at least, are not dealing with that. Oh, and you still have my mage. I'd like him to come home at some point."

"Oh, brother, stop with the whining. You've never been happier," I smiled even more broadly. "I like Taranath. I would like to keep him."

Brennan's answering smile told me that I was right. "This is true. So you've made up your mind? Shall I call Father? Or will you? Unless you need to wail and carry on some more? No amount of such noise will get you Taranath. He's on loan. Nothing more."

I could see the raised brow even through the mirror.

"Go away, lordship. I have things to do." I rolled my eyes in an exaggerated fashion so that he'd see me.

Then we laughed together, and the mirror winked out. I put it back in my pouch. I felt better than I'd felt since coming to the Dragon Realm.

Because at last, I could see where there was hope.

Granted, it was far in the distance. But it was there.

And I could live with that.

CHAPTER 6

*D*rake

The door burst open. It had to be Aine. She'd gotten into the habit of not knocking, and announcing herself via conversation. I felt a strong urge to be taking a bath so that she might learn others weren't waiting for her to come in and talk. But I hadn't managed to have that much time for myself yet when she tended to burst in.

I was glad, though, for the distraction. I didn't want to think about all the things I needed to address. Or anything at all. I was attempting to face all the things that had to be handled with a positive attitude, but towards midday, it sometimes became a challenge.

"How can I help you?" I asked dryly, wondering if she'd catch my tone.

"I need you to come with me right now," she said a little breathlessly.

No, she hadn't even noticed. "Are you all right?" I asked. "What have you been doing?"

"I ran all the way here," she inhaled deeply, then

continued. "I've been talking with Fangorn, and he'd like to meet with you."

I raised my eyebrows. This was something I could forgive her bursting in for. Jharak had become rather nagging in his requests that I meet with the dragon who was alert and awake down below the Dragon Castle, but he'd not wanted to meet with any fae up until now.

I understood. After the dragon wars, most of the dragons had been destroyed. Eleven remained, and of those eleven, only one was awake and sentient. That was Fangorn, who was also related to Aine via her parents. She'd told me some of it, and then handed me the journals that once belonged to Eilor, the former Dragon King. He'd written in great detail with regards to how Aine came to be. From what she'd told me, it was horrific. The man had been a cruel tyrant.

That was why I couldn't yell at Aine. I felt like the rest of the Fae Realm had let her down. Eilor had been doing all his dirty work right under our noses. Everyone in the Dragon Court knew who Aine was, although they didn't know the truth of *what* she was. Or where she'd come from. If they knew she was part dragon, and her ancestor was a dragon shifter, she wouldn't be safe. Fear of what the dragons had done in the Fae Realm was still very real.

"So this means you found the way down to the cavern?" The last time we'd talked about the dragons, she had not yet known how to get to them.

Aine nodded.

"When were you going to tell me?"

"Within the next week, regardless of how Fangorn felt about it. I have been taking the time to get to speak with him without any pressure, seeking nothing from him. You must understand, the only time he saw anyone was when they wanted something from him. I don't want to be one of those. So I waited."

Her eyes met mine. In them, I saw both regret at not telling me, and no regret at all. Again, I thought about how she carefully considered her actions. She was cautious but not overly so.

And she was probably right in her assessment here. I smiled. This was a good thing. "All right. Does he want anything in particular?" When she gave me an exasperated look, I held up my hands in defense. "I'm just asking! If there is something specific on the agenda, I'd like to be prepared."

Her shoulders relaxed as she searched my face, seeing the truth. Aine was even less trusting than I was, although you'd never know it from her reserved demeanor.

"He's in the mood to meet you. I don't know all his thoughts. I wouldn't say I know him well yet, but I think that if he's in the mood to be social, we shouldn't pass it up."

I liked that she said 'we'. Sometimes, the way she spoke of the dragons made me unsure exactly where she felt her loyalties fell. After all, she had one foot in each camp. She was dragon and fae.

"Lead on," I said.

I could feel the sweat running down my back. Why had I agreed to this again? Aine didn't seem bothered at all. Not one bit. It made me hate her a little. Which was petty, and unkind.

At the moment, I didn't care.

Prior to making our way down here, down the longest stairway I'd ever been on, she'd insisted on blindfolding me until we were partway down the stairs. I'd initially refused.

"I am not being blindfolded," I said, putting my hands on my hips.

"You are if you want to see the dragons," she shot back with no hesitation. "They have been used and treated poorly since the moment they were placed here. I am not going to be the one who gives the fae—any fae—that power ever again!"

"You are fae, Aine," I said.

"And I am also part dragon, and part human. What's to say I won't end up down here with the rest of them? No, Drake, you must trust me on this. I want the best for this Realm, but keeping the dragons as they are is not how we will achieve that. And as I am the only one who knows how to get to them, I will safeguard that. For them, and myself." She crossed her arms, and eyed me steadily.

I'd agreed. She was terrifyingly logical, and I couldn't fault her observations or her concerns. I didn't like them, but I couldn't fault them.

Which led me to the present.

A dragon—a real, live, capable-of-burning-me-with-a-hearty-breath dragon was staring me down. If he could have, I believe he would have crossed his arms.

Aine told me before we came to see him that I'd be able to see both fae and dragon in Fangorn.

"How in the name of the gods did he come to be a shifter?" I asked as she led me to wherever it was we were going.

"It's a long story, and it is not mine to share. Perhaps he will tell you if you ask nicely."

I had nothing to say to that. Aine carefully pulled me along, like a child on leading strings.

Another source of irritation—since she'd bullied me

into wearing the blindfold when she led me to the stairway, I couldn't find it if I'd tried. We'd come to a place in the castle that led to the rooms where Eilor, the former king, had lived. Aine had stopped then, and insisted I wear a blindfold. I was beginning to trust her, but this had almost been too much.

Only my father's words in my ear kept me from telling her exactly what she could do with the blindfold and storming off. If I was going to actually do this, if I was actually going to be the king of this blasted Realm, I would need to stop telling people where to go, or what to do with inanimate objects. I couldn't believe I was considering it, but I was.

Which led me here. Being eyed by a stern, big dragon.

"Why are you here, Drake, son of Jharak?" His voice rumbled.

The timbre of his voice was so deep I could feel it in my bones.

"I am here because your…" I stopped. What in the name of all the sun and stars was Aine to him? The sweat intensified. Which made me angry. He might be a dragon, I could end up as tonight's toasted snack, but I wasn't a stripling youth, hoping for a favor.

I began again. "I am here because my father requested that I see you when you were ready. Aine," I nodded to her, where she stood next to me silently, "Told me that today was the time for us to meet. As I am considering leading this Realm and seeing if I can repair the damage that has been done, I need to see all the things that are damaged." I crossed my arms, hoped that I wasn't sweating out anything he could smell, and gave him my own version of the stare-down.

I hoped I hadn't said the wrong thing.

Fangorn, the dragon in front of me, didn't move. Then

his nostrils flared—and I could tell, although I couldn't have told what moved exactly, that he relaxed.

I felt as though I had passed some sort of test.

"Son of Jharak, you are not what I expected. You are the human-born son of the King?"

I narrowed my eyes. Was he going to toss insults, see if he could make me angry?

"I am, Fangorn. Were you not aware of this?"

"Your coming to the Fae Realm happened after I was placed here," Fangorn responded mildly. "I only heard about it from the eldest son of Jharak, Cian. Or Kelan, as he was also known. He was fairly…" Fangorn paused.

I looked up, and was startled at the expression on his face. He was very much fae and dragon, and I could see both in his expression. He almost looked as though he was trying not laugh at the memory of Cian.

"Put out." Fangorn finally said.

I laughed in spite of myself. "That is, my lord, a perfect description of Cian. He was most definitely put out every time I saw him. I don't believe I ever saw him in any other mood!" I laughed again at the thought of bringing that angry man, filled with hate, down to a joke.

It was fitting. Cian deserved it.

Fangorn smiled. "I am glad that we are of the same mind. I understand from Aine that he is dead?"

"Very much so. I watched him die." I didn't bother hiding the satisfaction I felt as I spoke.

"Said like a good warrior," Fangorn said. "But is it what a good king would say?"

I'd been ready to thank him for the compliment, but now I was glad I'd not been able to. I knew a backhanded compliment when I heard one. I'd grown up in the Fae Court, where that was standard conversation.

I shrugged. He'd have to do better than that. "A good

king recognizes the positive aspects of an enemy being removed."

Fangorn's eyes narrowed, and I heard the intake of breath from Aine beside me. This wasn't how I wanted things to go, but I wasn't going to kowtow to this man or dragon, even if becoming a dragon meal was a possibility. Besides, I wasn't sure if he would be a friend or a foe, even though Aine felt he was a friend and an ally.

Better that we understood one another. No matter the outcome. I crossed my arms and gave him my own narrowed gaze, not letting my eyes shift from his.

"And Eilor? Where is he?" A gleam from his green eyes caught the light of the torches along the wall.

It must have been my imagination, but the torches seemed to glow more brightly, and I could smell the scent of whatever oil was on them. A burnt herbal smell. Then I wondered who—or what—oiled the torches down here. I forced myself back into the moment. I couldn't let my mind slip when dealing with a dragon.

"He hasn't been found yet, but we believe he is dead."

The dragon raised one brow ridge. How did he manage to look both fae and dragon at the same time?

"I would not make that assumption, son of Jharak."

"We are still searching for him, but would he still hide himself as his Realm is given away, his Castle plundered, as he would see it, and after knowing his daughter was killed?" I raised my own eyebrows.

Fangorn shrugged. "He and Ailla parted paths some time ago. He warned her that the path of the elder son of Jharak was a poor choice, but…" he shrugged again. "She would not listen. I think you need to ascertain that Eilor is, in fact, dead, before choosing another king, be it yourself or anyone else."

"Why?" I asked.

The conversation was clearly over, though. After he'd finished speaking, Fangorn turned and moved to the back of his cage, his back to where Aine and I stood.

"Thank you, Grandfather," Aine said.

I saw his shoulders move at her words, but he stayed where he was.

Aine touched me on the arm, and turned from the cage. "We should go now."

I didn't speak as we walked back up the stairs, lost in thought. What did Fangorn know? What was he not sharing? It was frustrating to come away from this meeting with as many questions as I'd had before I'd been able to meet him.

I stopped, putting my hand on Aine's arm. "Are you going to blindfold me again?"

She nodded. "Yes. I am sorry, and I don't mean to be rude, but I feel strongly that I must protect them. You've seen them. They're trapped. Fangorn has been made to do the bidding of Eilor for years. He's lost so much, not just his control, and—"

I held up a hand. "I understand. I just wanted to know if I should expect that you would lead me out of here."

She closed her mouth and looked at me with an expression I couldn't decipher. "Thank you," she said finally. She seemed as though she were in the middle of some emotional...thing.

Aine turned and began walking up the stairs again. Whatever was going on with her, she was choosing not to share.

Which was good. I didn't have the stamina for whatever it might be. Not right now. Fangorn's words played over and over in my head. *I think you need to ascertain that Eilor is, in fact, dead, before choosing another king, be it yourself or anyone else*. What did that mean? It felt like there was a lot behind it, that the words were a warning.

Why wouldn't he just spit it out, tell me? Damn dragons. Father had said they were wily.

I'd need to talk to Jharak. He would be thrilled I'd seen Fangorn, although maybe less so when I told him that nothing really had been settled. Or that the dragon's words had unsettled me further.

I sighed, thinking about that forthcoming conversation when Aine stopped.

"I need to blindfold you now," she said.

She still sounded apologetic.

I stood still and let her tie the cloth over my eyes. I could feel the warmth of her hands, and I was glad that she was being careful. I trusted her, but the fear of falling flat on my face loomed large when she took my hand.

"We're nearly at the top," she said. "Only about twenty more steps."

"That's not really at the top," I grumbled.

"Stop whining."

Annoying though it might be when directed at me, I liked her forthright manner. In that, Aine was a great deal like me. When she chose to be, anyway. She kept a lot to herself.

For the first time since I'd come here, I realized that I'd actually made some progress, and that there was hope to be found here.

CHAPTER 7

*a*ine

She watched Drake, bent over plans with the newly appointed steward of the household. He was figuring out where all the people who were coming to see his coronation were to be housed.

Aine wasn't sure what had happened, but in the course of the time where she avoided Drake, he had changed. Something had happened for him, something had taken all his concerns, and made them positive. By the time she'd brought him to see Fangorn, his entire attitude had shifted.

Now, when he walked through the castle, he stopped, and talked with people. Even walking through the castle was new. He didn't hide out in that little storeroom he called a study. She wasn't sure that he could see it, but the people who were formerly part of the court of King Eilor were beginning to trust him. She wasn't sure she was included in that trust, but no one was spitting on her, so she would count that as positive.

What she saw was the man she'd met in the castle

when he'd come to rescue his brother. Sarcastic, caring, and competent. Unafraid to face anything that came his way, no matter how large or small.

She was pleased to see it. She'd finished Eilor's journals, and what she'd read made her ill. More than once, she'd had to visit the necessary to throw up. How he could have done the things he'd done...it sickened her. His future plans, what he'd had in mind for her...she hoped he was dead, and that it had been slow, and painful. That he watched himself die.

She'd been talking more with Fangorn. Little by little, he was beginning to trust her as well. He wanted to. They were family, blood family. He wanted to be close to his family. She could feel the longing. But every time he told her more, told her the histories, it was difficult. Particularly as Eilor was so entwined in them. He'd changed the entire course of existence for the dragons.

Which meant that he would not give all this up, if he were still alive. Which also meant that things would be hard, regardless of the progress that had been made within the Realm. She needed to tell what she'd learned to Drake...but she didn't want to see him return to the angry man he'd been. Watching Drake face the challenges that awaited him head on only made her feel worse.

Because she knew what was still to come. It would keep...for now.

*D*rake
         I surveyed the room with satisfaction. I'd let Jharak know that I'd take this on. He'd immediately insisted on planning a big celebration. The fact that I wasn't interested wasn't even considered.

And my mother was coming.

But this would be my kingdom. For the first time since I'd come here, I had a sense of the peace that could happen. It would not be easy, and this Realm promised to be surly, and full of secrets, and squabbling.

Meeting with Fangorn, however, had changed things. I didn't know why, and I didn't even know how to bring it up to Aine, or Fangorn, but it had.

I felt more…accepted. Which made no sense, and had no logic behind it. That was, however, how I felt.

The problem of not being sure where Eilor was continued to be a thorn in my side. Fangorn was insistent that he and the other dragons would be free, that their cages would open, once Eilor was dead.

He did not specify as to how he knew, but he was certain.

I would believe him until something proved otherwise. That did not, however, stop me from speaking with Taranath on how one might open the cages.

This room, the Great Hall, had been swept, and aired, and cleaned until there was no trace of the former king. The people that were moving through here on various errands had a slightly more hopeful demeanor than I'd seen previously.

I could do this.

Which meant I'd have to tell my father—and Brennan —that they'd been right.

I sighed. A small price to pay.

The future, for the first time, had a different cast for me.

"Aine?"

"Yes?" She was there, at my side.

"Will you come with me? I need to contact the Fae King."

Her eyes met mine, and she smiled. "Of course."

I returned the smile, and together, we walked toward my study. It was time.

"Long live the Dragon King," Aine said softly.

A FINAL NOTE

DRAKE'S DILEMMA and AINE'S TALE take place around the same time. They finish in RISE OF THE DRAGON KING. These two Tales are, more than the others, meant to be read with one of the main novels.

Drake and Aine surprised me, because I had no intention of them being more than secondary characters. But when I learned Aine's story, and that Drake would be the Dragon King, their stories just exploded.

So enjoy.

CIAN'S TALE

A Realm Companion Story
Tale #6

To all the villains I've met...
inspiration has been a silver lining.

AUTHOR'S NOTE

CIAN'S TALE is the sixth short story in the Realm Companion Tales. It's the story of Cian, the eldest son of Jharak and Nerida. We heard what happened to him in **BROTHERS BORN**, when he and Brennan got into an argument. This story picks up after Cian is removed from the Fae Castle. That scene was shared in **BROTHERS BORN** when Brennan is standing with Nerida watching Cian being carried away.

If you've read the other Realm novels, then you will know Cian is really…crazy. He has a ton of baggage (who doesn't, right? But he *really* needs some baggage management skills…) and he is attempting to exorcise the things he's carried—make them right for him. This will cover his life from the time he is taken away until the end. It went places I didn't expect— he's probably the worst of the bad guys I've written.

This story came out of wanting to know how Cian went from the bratty kid he was to a full-fledged homicidal power monger. Complete with a harem. There's gotta be a story there.

And here it is.

Lisa

PROLOGUE

Excerpt from BROTHERS BORN
Brennan

*B*rennan didn't understand it. He didn't want to be the Goblin King, but he knew he had to train for it. Just as Cian trained to be the Fae King. Why Cian had taken such a dislike to his brother having a throne—especially as it was not as good as the Fae throne, Brennan didn't know.

That morning, in the garden, when Cian made fun of him as he often did now and called him a little goblin, he felt his temper rise up. It felt alive, as though he, Brennan, didn't have control over it anymore. He was fae, just as Cian was. He was not a goblin!

He did something that he and his instructors had been working on. He wished for his brother to feel the pain he inflicted. He wished for his brother to know how mean his words were, how hurtful. And he wished for his brother to stop, to just be quiet.

Cian became quiet. From that day onward, Cian never said a word again.

Brennan remembered as he watched from his mother's side as the body of Cian was taken away. His eyes hot and dry. No one spoke to him unless they had to. He spent his time in his chambers, or with his tutors.

And he missed his brother.

At night, he let the tears fall. Fae did not cry. Rather, they weren't supposed to. That's what he'd been taught. Even as they'd watched Cian being taken away, his mother hadn't cried outside of the one solitary tear. Tears were not supposed to come easily for the fae. Did this, in, fact make him more like a goblin? They were often less disciplined and controlled in their emotions, a fact which Cian did not allow him to forget.

When Cian lived.

He'd killed his brother.

He would never get past the fact. Cian was dead and gone, and it was Brennan's fault.

CHAPTER 1

$\mathcal{I}$ woke, unsure as to where I was. It wasn't my room. I didn't see all the tapestries and fine things that adorned my quarters.

I was in a plain white room, a servant's room. There were tall windows across the bed from me, and they were open about a third of the way. The curtains, which were pale cream and gossamer, floated back and forth in the breeze.

Still a servant's room.

I sat up, intending to find out what was going on, and why I was here, rather than my own familiar quarters.

Just as I opened my mouth to yell for one of my staff, a woman popped out from one of the curtains. Looking beyond her, I saw that a rocking chair was positioned there.

It was my nurse, my old Nanny. She was still in the castle, but I hadn't seen her up close, or in my rooms, in years. I was nearly too old for a nanny. I had a staff, and manservants to help me bathe, and dress, as befitted the next Fae King. Not a nanny.

"My boy! My sweet boy! You're awake!" She moved towards him with hands outstretched.

I was so shocked I allowed her to approach me, and even take my face in her hands and plant kisses upon my forehead. Kisses were something I deserved, not only from my nanny, but everyone else. Although it was odd to get them from the nanny I rarely saw anymore.

"Where are my parents? Where are the king and queen?" I asked, my tone imperious.

Margot pulled her hands back toward herself, finally, and covered her mouth with them. Her eyes almost looked like she might start to cry, but that could be. Fae did not cry. Ever. It was a sign of weakness, perhaps a sign of weak blood. I did not have weak blood. Nanny might, but I did not.

"Oh, my sweet boy, they are not here." She said. The words were soft, but the meaning was not. The truth was hard and not very forgiving.

I threw back the blankets, and set my feet up on the floor, looking for my slippers. I looked down, and noticed my clothing were not the normal silk pajamas I prefer to wear to bed.

"Where my appropriate nightclothes? Where my slip-pers? And where are we? Why am I not in my rooms? Why have I been moved?"

Nanny did not answer me. Instead, amazingly, she turned and went to her rocking chair, picking it up. She came back towards the bed, still holding the chair, and then set it down. She sat in it, and smiled at me, but her smile was tinged with sadness. Anyone could see that.

It wasn't appropriate. Servants did not look at me like that. Not even Nanny. Not ever.

My patience snapped. "Nanny! I demand that you tell me what is going on!"

Nanny only smiled at me, and then she clapped her hands, looking towards the door. Another servant came in, and she whispered something to it and he ran off again closing the door quietly behind him.

"I have ordered you something to eat, a light broth, and something to drink. You've been asleep for some time." She looked at me fondly.

More fondly than I ever remembered her looking at me. If I wasn't mistaken, she was crying! Fae didn't cry. And servants didn't cry in front of their masters.

This was getting ridiculous. "Why have I been asleep? Where am I? What happened? Where are my parents, and why am I—" I looked around in disgust. "Here?"

Then I thought back to the last thing I remembered.

The garden. I was in the garden. We were playing camogh, and Brennan, that whiny sniveler, had the nerve to ask if he could join our game. Of course I had said no, and looking like a goblin that someone had kicked, he slunk off behind the bushes. I remembered that I had returned to the game, and then — I remembered no more.

I looked at Nanny, my eyes accusing. "What happened to me? What did that little sniveling rat of a brother do to me? Where are my parents, Nanny?"

"Oh, my dear Lord Cian, my sweet boy, they've sent you away."

I stared at her, open mouth. Thankfully, I recovered quickly. "What you mean, they've sent me away? I am the heir to the Fae Realm! They can't send me away!"

Nanny looked down at her clasped hands in her lap, and she nodded. "Yes, my Lord, they can. They are the king and queen. They can do whatever it is they please."

"Who will take over the Fae Throne?" I asked, even though I was afraid I Arity knew the answer.

"Why, your brother." Nanny's voice was innocent, her eyes wide.

I could feel my palm start to itch, and my temper rare up inside of me like a towering mountain, a raging sea. Father had taken me to see the sea. One time, on the edge of the Dwarf Realm. It was a stormy day, and the waves crashed up along the beach, and I could see the sand shift and move every time the waves came up to the beach.

I was those waves. I only wanted to crash and destroy and hurt everyone and everything that it put me here.

My brother first among those on the list.

———

I'd fallen back onto my bed, trying to keep my anger contained. My parents had sent me away! For what? For not lying about my brother? For not wanting to be around someone who was going to live out his life with goblins? Who would want to be around that? No one I knew.

Nanny left me alone, but finally, she spoke. "My Lord, you must keep up your strength." She still spoke in the same soft tone she'd been using since I woke.

Food was brought up, and while I ate, Nanny told me what had happened. She told me that my parents had put it about that I had died. I'd collapsed when Brennan attacked me, and I didn't wake up. So they didn't want me around anymore. Nanny cried when she told me that.

When she told me the truth. The truth was they had sent me off to one of their small, remote castles. She told me that she had begged to come along with me, so that I might not be tended to by people who did not know me. People who do not love me. In that moment, I was profoundly grateful for her. Even if she was only a servant.

How had it come to pass that a servant was more loyal than my own parents? My own mother? I thought she loved me.

But she sent me away, at the first sign of trouble from my pathetic brat of a brother.

Then she told me the worst thing of all. My parents had brought another child into their home. Nanny told me it was the talk of all of the Realm. Of all the Realms. A child had been wished away to the Goblin King. Some whelp from the Human Realm. A whelp who should die. Humans weren't good enough to be in the Fae Realm. They were as bad as goblins, or the wolf-people. Looking to replace me, my mother had brought the child home to the Fae Castle, and introduced him to my traitorous, sneaking brother.

Nanny reported that the two of them got along as though they were true brothers. As though Brennan had not killed his only brother. Nanny told me that the entire Realm, thought I was dead. And that they all thought Brennan had done it.

But there he was, still in the castle, still heir to the goblin throne.

I remembered what I'd overheard. When my parents were talking, when they didn't think that anyone was around. That Brennan was special, and because of that, he needed to be nurtured; those were my mother's words. He needed to be nurtured. And then she told my father that they would need to take special care with him, and of him.

Even remembering it, even though it was over a year ago, it still made my blood burn.

No one wanted to be the Goblin King. Goblins were nasty, stinky, horrid little creeping things. They weren't fae, weren't even on the same level as fae. Why there was an entire realm devoted to them, I didn't know. But then we had a Troll Realm, and a Dwarf Realm. I'd never seen a troll, and only a few dwarves had come to the Fae Castle. The trolls and dwarves tended to keep to themselves. At least the dwarves produced amazing gems. I looked down at my hands. I had rings from the Dwarf Realm, given to me when my father announced that I was his heir.

My rings were gone

Along with my fine clothing. And my rooms. And my place within my world. Gone. It was all gone. "Why?" I yelled getting out of bed, and throwing the bowl of soup that Nanny had had brought for me. "Why? Why did they do this to me?"

Nanny glided in from the other room. I didn't realize she was there.

As though I wasn't shouting aloud, she said, "I am sure I do not know, my Lord," her face showing her sadness. "I am but a nursery maid, and kings and queens do not share the reasons with such as me. I did however," a nervous looking over her face, as though she did not wish to tell me the rest.

"Go on, I said.

"I did hear the King tell the Queen that sending you away was all for the best," she said. "That it would allow your brother to heal."

This time it was a cup that flew across the room. They sent me away, and told everyone I was dead? So that Brennan might feel better?

"Well, that's just not going to stand. Come, Nanny, let us ready me for travel. I am going home."

"Oh, my Lord, I would do so, but…" She looked down at her hands again. "I am afraid that everyone thinks you are dead. No one will believe you should you try to go back and claim to be Cian, son of the Fae King. They have already had a funeral for you."

I sat down on the bed. They had held a funeral for me? They thought I was dead?

For the first time since I'd awoken, I felt the weight of all that I've learned sit upon me. "Nanny, what am I to do? Where am I to go?" I hated how weak I sounded, but I honestly did not know what was to happen next. I had been disowned by my own parents.

Nanny got up from her chair, and came to kneel next to me where I sat on the bed. She classed my hands, and held it to her cheek. "My lord, I have an idea. This will allow us to live in peace where we cannot be found by your parents."

"Are we sure it would not be better to go to my parents?" I asked in a small voice.

"No, my lord, I do not believe it would be. They have taken pains to pretend that you have died. For you to return — I'm afraid it would mean your death for real." She took my hands, and held it to her cheek.

I looked down at her dark hair, neatly parted and pulled back into a bun as it had been every day since I could remember. She loved me. She would take care of me. She wouldn't let anything happen to me.

She was the only person who did. She was all I had left.

"Very well, Nanny. Would you please share with me your idea?" With a smile, she sat next to me on the bed. She even put her arm around me. Normally I would've rebuked her for such a privilege, but instead I leaned against her, enjoying the smell of bread that rose from her clothing, and the warmth that her body and her arm around provided. I didn't realize until this moment how much I miss my parents, my mother.

But at least Nanny would be here for me.

I stood behind Nanny, dressed plainly and simply, as a son of a former nanny would be. We had traveled many days to the Dragon Realm. She had requested an audience with Eilor, the Dragon King. I had never met him, but I heard he was a very proud man. I was very surprised when her audience was granted. She had told me to come with her, and an uncharacteristically stern tone told me to cover my head and look for all the world as though I was the simple son of a nanny, afraid to look anyone in the eye, and happy just to be here.

She must've seen the look on my face, because she quickly hurried to say, "My lord, you will not always need to hide. But for now, while I secure a place for us, and for your safety, you must do as I say."

It rankled me to take orders from someone who was a member of my nursery staff. But her words made sense. They had logic. And she was the only person willing to stand by me.

So here I stood, nearly supplicating like a beggar, in front of someone who was, at the very least, my equal. My father was the Fae King. And the Fae King ruled over all. I was—or at least, I had been—his heir. So it rankled to take a knee for the Dragon King.

But I did it, for Nanny, and for myself. Mostly for myself. While I listened to the murmur of her voice, I vowed revenge on every single person that had brought me to this place. To a place where I had to dress as one who was lowly, and bow to another king. *I* was King. I was the king who was to rule over all the kings. I would never forget this. Not ever.

"Nanny," said the deep voice of Eilor, "it is with great affection that I received your message. What brings you, would give me the great luck of having you, back into the Dragon Realm?"

"My son and I, we are no longer welcome in the Fae Court. With the loss of my charge," here Nanny looked up at the Dragon King, and they met one another's eyes for a long period of time, "I was let go. I have wandered for some time, with my son. I have come to ask, might you be needing some help in the nurseries? If I recall correctly, your Majesty, you have a fine daughter, close to the age of my son."

"I do. Indeed, my dear Nanny. I do indeed. I believe that we have a place for you. You and your son. You took such good care of me all those years ago, you can surely do no less for my daughter. We will be pleased to have you."

I chanced a look up then. Eilor was staring down at me, a smile on his face. Perhaps the old Dragon King is not as bad as I had heard.

At least we would have a place to live, and I wouldn't be covered in filth anymore. A castle, with good food, clothing, and baths. It wouldn't be the same. Nothing would ever be the same. But it would be better.

And I would have my revenge.

CHAPTER 2

We had been some time in the Dragon Room. Eilor, the king, had come to me a few days after we got there, and asked if he could speak with me, man-to-man. Of course I agreed. He asked me to come with him, and I followed.

He led me to a walkway atop the battlements of the castle. Clasped his hands behind his back, he looked out over the Dragon Realm.

"Are you happy here, Cian?"

I stopped, my heart pounding. Nanny and I had agreed it would tell no one my name. How was it that the King do? I looked at him, my eyes wide. Fear making my mouth dry.

"How—how do you know to call me—that is not my name! My name is Kelan, and I am the son of Nanny! I— I am not—" I was so shocked, I couldn't speak clearly. Nanny had made sure that I knew what awaited me if my true name was revealed. I would be hunted, taken back to the Fae Castle.

Put to death for real this time.

To my surprise, the king began to laugh. "Not many know who you truly are, but I am more aware of what goes on in all the Realms than most," he said. "When Nanny told me that your name was Kelan I was happy to go along with it. But you've got to get better about answering to the name, Kelan. You hesitate in that moment before you respond. It makes people suspicious."

I finally found my voice, and said, "What are you going to do? Are you going to send me back to my parents?" I wanted to go home more than anything, but I knew that home was lost to me forever. For a moment, my hatred of Brennan burned brightly. It was his fault. If it wasn't for him, my parents wouldn't have sent me away. It all went back to Brennan. And that he was special, and I was not. If it weren't for him, I wouldn't be here. Not like this. I'd be where I belonged.

The king stopped laughing and turned towards me, his face serious. "No, Kelan. I am not. As far as the world knows, you have only one parent. And that is Nanny. I'm going to allow her to raise you, with my daughter Ailla. I'm going to ask that you do not reveal your identity to anyone. I know who you really are, Nanny knows who you are, but I would prefer to keep it between the three of us. If anyone else were to know, it would put all of us a danger. Do you not agree?"

I like that he was talking to me, as one king to another. He didn't talk to me like a child, or talk down to me like I couldn't understand what he was saying. I have been declared my father's heir at an early age, and I begin to pay attention, study how he acted, and attempt to be like him. I would've been a great King. If only it had not been stolen from me. If only my parents had not turned against me.

But here, in front of me, was a king who was treating

me as his equal, and giving me the respect and courtesy of another king.. As the young man who would've been his ruler. Eilor was a good man, I decided. He didn't behave inappropriately, or toss over the order of things to get what he wanted.

"I agree, your majesty."

He held up a hand. "Let us not stand on formality, Kelan. I will call you Kelan, and you may call me Eilor. I do ask that you do so only when we are alone. But when we are alone, there is no need to maintain formality. Because I knew who you are, and who you should be." And then, standing at the top of the battlements, with the sun in the distance, Eilor, King of the Dragon Room, bowed his head to me. As he might've done were I actually on the throne, as the Fae King.

"Thank you, Eilor. That is most generous of you," I said. "And I agree to your terms. It will keep us all safe," I added.

Eilor smiled, and I felt the approval of a parent for the first time. It seemed like a long time since I'd felt that way. Nanny loved me, but it wasn't the same. Part of me knew I was not being kind to her. She put me first in all of her considerations. But in that moment, I felt a pang for my mother, my father. Flashes of them passed through my mind's eye, smiling at me, hugging me, laughing with me, even laughing with my brother. I would never see them again. From now until the time I died, no one would ever know who I really was. From now until forever more, I would be Kelan. Son of the nanny, Margot.

For the first time in my life, I felt the hot, itchy feeling in my eyes that indicated there may actually be tears there. I never cried before. I'd heard of it, and taunted those that I caught crying mercilessly. It was deserved. But now, here I was, nearly crying in front of a king. Worse, it was the one king who treated me as his equal. Over parents that treated me as nothing. Who were always on at me to be more kind to others, especially to that traitor Brennan. Who lectured me about learning and reading more, doing my magic, always putting others first. That the Realm took precedence over us all.

When it came to it, they had not acted in the best interests of the Realm. They had acted in the best interests of one child. One child over the other. Who would rule the Fae Realm now? Brennan? The thought almost made me laugh. As if he could manage anything, the little worm.

I looked over the battlements, at the Dragon Realm, and wiped at my face as though I were just scrubbing the tired off of it. I made sure to remove any traitorous tears that might be attempting to make an appearance.

My face calm, I turned towards the Dragon King. "I am in your debt, Eilor," I said.

He smiled broadly. "I think we should continue our walk now. We shall consider this a relationship of equality and barter, Kelan. I think you're going to be a valuable asset to my court."

I threw the ewer across the room. It hit the wall, and slid to the ground with a resounding, satisfying crash.

Nanny glared at me, hands on her hips. "You can't go about doing that, as you did once before! This is not the same place for us, and it is not safe for you to...to act as you were." She said to me, her voice almost inaudible.

Nanny had become quite familiar since we moved into the Dragon Realm. She spoke to me almost as a mother would. I suppose it was necessary, as that was the ruse that we were enacting, but she didn't have to keep it up. We were alone, behind closed doors. I didn't think I needed to hide who I was, or how I felt particularly when I'd heard such disgusting news.

"What is it that's got you all bother?" Nanny asked.

"Have you heard?" I yelled at her.

"No K — my lord," she amended quickly when she saw the look on my face. "I've heard nothing that I can see as the reason for this rage. Would you be willing to share your news with me?"

Her formality eased a small part of my rage. But only a small part. "My parents — my real parents — they have adopted another son! Ailla told me about it today! She overheard her father talking, and she wanted to tell me about it." The boy, the one from the Human Realm— they'd adopted him. Given him my place.

To my surprise, Nanny did look angry. She was not outraged on my behalf, which I thought she would be for sure. Instead, her face went white, and she looked afraid.

"Why… Why do you think she would tell you that, Kelan?" Her voice shook, and she seemed afraid.

I shrugged. "I don't know, she wanted to share something that she overheard. It's fun to talk about the things that people don't think children should hear. Why?" A new thought entered my mind. "Do you think she knows?" I wanted to tell her that I was Cian, and I was not the son of the nanny, the boy she sneered at and talked down to when she was angry. Or when she felt like it.

"Oh, heavens, no! If she knew, we would have to leave, Kelan! There would be no way that we could stay! The King has been most clear that no one is to know who you really are, other than you and him and me! Please, tell me you haven't told her!" Nanny came over to me, and knelt down in front of me clasping my hands.

I looked down at her bowed head, remembering that she was the only one that stayed with me, the only one that stuck with me that stood next to me stood behind me stood with me when my own parents cast me out. I gently removed my hands from hers, not wanting to hurt her feelings. But I didn't wish to be pawed over like some sobbing, snotty child.

"I have told her nothing, and I doubt that she suspects. She's only a little girl, after all," I said a little scornfully. Ailla was sweet, and I love that she adored me—well, most of the time, but she was a girl. And a short one at that.

She was the only person who would play with me, though. All the boys of the castle, the sons of the various lords and ladies of the court didn't see me as their equal. I was the nursemaid's son, and not worth playing with. Even though I was a better swordsman than most of them. I understood the need for secrecy, but their blatant disrespect and sometimes open jeers angered me. I long to tell them who I really was, but I knew I could not.

For as Nanny had told me, and Eilor had affirmed, my parents told everyone I was dead. Were I to appear now, they would not be able to acknowledge me. They would kill me, rather than have their lie exposed.

And so I put up with the taunts of those who were lesser than me, out of concern for myself and the people who love me, and who I cared for in return.

I stood among the group of people in the hall, watching as the former Goblin Queen bowed low before Eilor.

When she stood, however, she was tall and straight. Her voice was strong, and she did not mince words, or stumble in any fashion. I found her to be a very admirable woman. In spite of the fact that she'd been forced to live in that filthy Goblin Realm for years. I'm sure the loss of her husband was painful, but a part of me believed that she ought to be thanking my brother for getting her out of that Realm. The only good thing about knowing that he was the King of the Goblin Realm was that he would have to be King of the Goblin Realm. He would no longer be in the Fae Realm, in the luxury and beauty of the Fae Castle.

And yet still, it rankled. My brother, the sniveling weasel, the slinking would-be goblin, was now a king. And yet I've stayed hidden, hidden among the common of this court, as though I were nothing. To all of them, I was nothing. I was the son of the nursemaid. The nursemaid who was getting old, and frail. I'd learned, since we had come here, that not only was Eilor happy to have her help to raise his daughter, Margot had in fact been his nursemaid.

She looked old, but not that old.

"I am pleased at your offer of shelter, and sanctuary. My Realm has been stolen from me, as has my husband, the Goblin King. My daughter, Princess of the Goblin Realm, and I are at your mercy, and we thank you for your hospitality." With that, the former queen of the Goblin Realm curtsy low to the entire court of the Dragon Realm. Her daughter followed suit behind her.

Eilor got up, clapping. It was obvious he was impressed with the strength and the show of the queen. I recalled that he had not had a queen, or even a consort in a long time. Ailla had told me that her mother had passed away when she was born, and no woman had emerged. Since then, as a mother. Perhaps Eilor looked on the former Goblin Queen as a potential mate?

To what end?

As I was thinking these thoughts, I happened to catch the eye of her daughter, the Princess Dhysara. Upon meeting my eye, she smiled, carefully, almost fearfully.

Something about her smile warmed the inside of me. As far as she knew, I was nothing but a common man of the court, nothing special, no lord, no titles. Yet she smiled at me as though I was. I felt my shoulders straightened, and I stood taller.

Her smile widened and then she cast her eyes downward, and followed her mother out of the throne room.

The Princess Dhysara was a very pretty girl.

CHAPTER 3

I paced back and forth in my quarters, unable to sit still, to sit down, to do anything. The old Goblin Queen had finally passed away, and her daughter, the Princess Dhysara, had asked to be sent somewhere else. She said she could no longer be where she and her mother had lived their last years and the place where she lost her mother.

I didn't understand wasting so much time on grief, but I respected Dhysara. I wanted to support her. But I didn't want her to go away.

Now that Ailla was grown, she no longer followed me around with the worshipful adoration. She had before. Oh, she still loved to talk—to tease me, flirting outrageously with me. Eilor always cautioned me against feeling too much for his daughter, as if I would. But he seemed to think that it would be a mistake on my part, versus one on hers.

Besides, I'd heard the rumors. They had been confirmed by Nanny, as well. Even old, infirm, and unable to leave her bed, Nanny was still a font of gossip. Now that

I was grown, she and I often sat and talked about what my next move should be, on how I could best leverage myself within the court. After all these hundreds of years, I had kept my cover as Kelan, son of the nursemaid.

I had smiled behind my hand at the jealous whispers of those who did not understand why the royal family favored me so. The Goblin Princess favored me as well. Which is why I was so upset that Dhysara would be leaving.

Once all the funeral proceedings had concluded, Dhysara had sought me out in the library.

"I want to tell you, Kelan. Before I told anyone else," she began. "I will soon be leaving."

I said down the book of spells I had been studying, and looked at her. "Why would you wish to do that?"

She took one of my hands in both of hers, and looked into my eyes. I could see a pleading within. "Now that my mother has gone, I have no wish to live here, depending on the charity of another king. I should have my own king-dom, and I do not. I must accept that. But I don't have to live here as an object of pity, and scorn. Dependent on the charity of another. I won't do it, Kelan! You of all people should understand that!"

"What you mean?" I asked carefully. This was danger-ously close to exposing an idea that I might not be who I said I was. I'd been too careful all these years to let it slip now. Even with my affection for Dhysara.

"You hold yourself like a king, and you behave better than most of lords in this court. You are the confidant of the King, the friend of the Princess, and even a friend to the lowly me," she said blushing as she cast her eyes down-ward. "There are many who are jealous of what they think you have," she looked up at me.

I resisted the urge to roll my eyes at her dramatics, and instead put a smile upon my face covering her hands with my other one. "I care not for what others say. I am content with those in my life whom I love, and who love me."

The blush deepened further upon her cheeks. The rosy color made her look very young, younger than she was.

"I… I do love you, Kelan," she said softly.

She was the first person other than Nanny who told me that she loved me, in over six hundred years. Ailla would never say such a thing, and Eilor certainly wouldn't. I was surprised to see how deeply I felt those words. How much I had missed hearing those words. I gazed into her eyes, seeing them shine up at me as though I held the moon and stars, and all I had to do was reach out and grab them to gift them to her.

I decided that was what I wanted. Someone who would look at me like that, and see no reason why I couldn't do it.

"Dhysara, my love, you marry me?"

"*Y*ou did what?" Ailla screamed at me.

"I am married, my lady," I said formally. I kept my smirk to myself. My calm demeanor made her anger far more enjoyable.

"You married that mewling, simpering goblin girl?"

"I must ask you, my lady, to be respectful of my wife."

"You arrogant, despicable man!" She screamed, moving quickly over towards her dressing table.

I had come to give her the news myself. Dhysara, delighted to have been married, no longer wished to stay in the Dragon realm. I felt it only right to let my oldest friend know that I was now leaving.

And it was turning out even better than I expected. It was delightful to see Ailla get so angry. This is what she got, this is what she deserved for being so hateful to me all those years. Teasing me, taunting me, flirting with all those other men of the court, the sad, pathetic little boys. They had nothing on me. Now she would know what it felt like. Now she would understand how hurtful it was. I hope she choked on her rage.

Quick as lightning, she snatched up something from her table, and threw it at me. I didn't move fast enough, which was unusual for me. I normally had very quick reflexes. The object — it was a mirror — hit me in the face, and shattered as it struck my cheek. I felt shards of glass cut my face from my eye down towards the bottom of my chin. The blood begin to drip down my face, and it felt like heavy rain down one side of my cheek.

I could feel the ache where the mirror hit me. And I could tell just by the way my cheek felt that there was still glass within the wound. I would need to have someone else, a mage, perhaps, remove all the glass. More than anything, I couldn't believe that Ailla struck me, hurt me. That I was *bleeding*.

"Go, go! Go to your little sniveling bride. And know this, Kelan! While you live in whatever hovel the two of you manage, I shall be living as the Goblin Queen!" She laughed when she saw the expression on my face.

"Oh, did you not know?" Her voice changed, became softer, more conversational. As though we were talking easily over a meal. "My father has betrothed me to Brennan, the king of the Goblin Realm. And the *only*," she drawled the word "natural son of the Fae King. Father feels that when Jharak is no longer king, Brennan, my intended, shall be. What have you to say now, Kelan?"

I would not give Ailla the satisfaction of knowing that she had hurt me. Even as I stood here dripping blood in her chambers. I hoped it stained the floor. I hoped that she would be unable to remove it. I murmured a spell to insure that the blood would never wash away. So that every time she saw it, every time that she was screaming at some serving girl to remove it, she would be reminded always at her cruelty to me. She would not be able to ignore it as she did the rest of the things she didn't wish to see.

Then I bowed, and looked up at her while I spoke. "Only that, as your old friend, I wish you well. I wish you much happiness with your husband."

I bowed deeper, allowing a stronger stream of blood to drip onto her floor. As I stood, I refused to touch the wound on my face. But I did allow my eyes to look at her in the most mocking manner. She glared, hands on her hips. She didn't know. She didn't know.

The fear that initially shot through me at her words eased. Even now, I could see Margot's white face when she feared my identity was known. Ailla was baiting me, taunting me like she always did. She knew, although not my reasons why, that I thought little of the Goblin King, and less of his adopted human brother. I would not play this game with her. She would not have that power over me. Carefully, I spoke, keeping my tone mild even as blood fell down onto my clothing. "I'm sorry I displease you, my lady. I will remove myself from your presence."

I turned and made for the door. But I didn't make it. I felt her hand on my arm, jerking me around, and that her hands on my face, regardless of the blood dripping down my cheek. She pulled my face towards hers, and kissed me hard. Ferociously, with a flame and a passion that I hadn't known she had. The interest, the flirtation — that had always been there. But this was something deeper, a fire that stirred the fire in my own loins. Fire that my new bride did not ignite.

I pulled her to me, and devoured her mouth. All these years, all this flirtation, and she waits until now, after I've married, to make her true feelings known. Even though I'd always suspected, she'd never said anything. Never!

Anger licked at the edges of my thoughts even as I lost myself in the desire for her. I kissed along the side of her neck, making sure to nip as I did so. I heard her little gasps that indicated she felt the scouring of my teeth.

I traced my hands along the edge of her bodice, and then when I came to the center, above her breasts, I yanked, hard. The shimmering fabric gave way, exposing her pert breasts. She had rose-colored nipples. They stood out in high relief against her skin. I grabbed her breasts with both hands and kneaded them roughly. She let her head tilt back and moaned.

I looked at the compliant woman in my hands. She should have been mine all along. The Goblin Princess was a fine bride for the heir to the Fae Throne. The Dragon Princess would have been even more fitting. Yet Ailla had refused to tell me the truth, choosing instead to play games.

She would never tell me no again. Not ever. She would learn that, right now.

I bent my head to her breasts, and took one of them in my mouth. I used my teeth to suck and then bite at her nipple. I let my hands drift down to the torn bodice, and not stopping my actions, tore it open further, exposing even more of her. She wrapped her arms around my head, pulling me closer, encouraging every bite, every lick, and every graze of my teeth. Each time she did so, I increased my intensity, feeling more and more ferocious each moment.

I was wild with desire for her, and at the same time I wanted to devour her. To hurt and bruise her, so that she would not forget to whom she belonged, what I was due. To mark her, to make sure that she never, ever, played games with me again. To make sure she knew that she was mine. And that she would never taunt me, tease me, or say no to me ever again. My breath was ragged, and it was hard to keep my thoughts in order.

When I had torn her clothing, rending it completely in half, I yanked it off of her so that she stood before me naked and exposed. She met my gaze with a bold look. One eyebrow cocked up in invitation. Her chest was flushed from my ministrations.

I stood up, and wrapped my fingers in her hair, pulling her to me. She stumbled a little but I ignored it. She needed to learn. I kissed her with the ferocity that I felt, the flames in my body reaching higher and higher. She moaned into my lips.

I slid my free hand down her body, enjoying the feel of her skin. When I reached her hip, I moved my hand abruptly between her legs, plunging it into her, ignoring her gasp. Back and forth, back and forth, until she was panting with each breath, and leaning against me for support.

"Ohhh," she said, her eyes closed, her head falling to the side.

I wasn't sure, but I thought she might be close to release. That would never do. If she were to get that from me, it would be on my terms. When I allowed it.

I let go of her hair, and removed my hand from between her legs. When I did so, I pushed her, just a little, away from me. She nearly lost her balance, but caught herself in time to keep from falling.

I bowed once more. "My lady Ailla," I said in a mocking tone. "You seem to have had an accident to your clothing."

She opened her mouth to speak, but I turned and headed for the door. I would not let her master me. Not even now, when I ached for her, when I was so hard that my breeches felt strained and I thought I might burst. I opened the door, and slipped out quickly. It was just in time. I heard something crash and hit the door behind me. That made me smile. It also removed the black cloud that her revelations had dropped on my head. To think that Ailla would be marrying my brother—

But I couldn't go on like this. I looked to the left and the right, looking for release. I headed towards my rooms, hoping I would encounter someone along the way. Anyone, anything to help me.

I healed my wound from Ailla as I walked. I'd been shocked, not thinking correctly. All this time, Eilor had been tutoring me in the ways of the magic of this realm. It was different than what I'd learned with my masters in the Fae Realm. The Dragon Realm had its own magic. Had I not been so taken aback at Ailla actually daring to hurt me, I would have remembered that sooner. Of course I could heal myself. There was no need for any other mage. I would never need another mage again.

By the time I reached my chambers. I could feel that the skin had knitted itself together once more, although I could not guarantee it would be the most attractive healing. Just as I put my hand on the handle of my door, a serving girl came around the corner carrying a basket of laundry. She was headed for my rooms.

Perfect. I smiled at her, and she faltered in her step. I opened the door, stepping inside and holding it open wider for her. "You've come just in time," I said. And closed the door behind her.

CHAPTER 4

I looked down to Brennan, strapped on the table in front of me. Everything, everything began with Brennan. All his sniveling, all his crying, all of his demands on my parents, it had ended with me, banished, scarred, unable to declare myself as who I really was. Unable to take what was rightfully mine. Forced to slink about in corners, like a stray animal hoping for the scraps from the tables of others.

From the tables of those lesser than me.

"Oh, how I've waited for this, brother," I sneered at the last word. "Let's talk, shall we?"

When he would not answer my questions, it was with great enjoyment that I listened to the sounds of his pain with the newest magic that I have learned. Magic that I learned in spite of Eilor—magic he had, and didn't want to share. Dragon magic. I'd never felt anything else like it.

I smiled. This was going to be a good day.

The day I had mastered Ailla, that had been another day like this. I'd waited for her for years, wanting her, burning for her, forced to exercise my want and need with the serving girls, who didn't deserve me. But while I suspected her feelings, I couldn't be sure. I would never, as she needled and taunted me, let her know how I felt.

When I'd learned she'd wanted me, it was the best feeling I'd ever experienced.

Until now.

Now, Brennan lay here, at my mercy. Just when he'd gotten what he thought he always wanted. I'd heard the tales. He was married. He and my father and their human born adopted whelp were some great trio, bent on helping and improving all the Realms.

"How is your lovely human-born, wife, brother? She must be quite a woman to attract the attention of a fae man with many women to choose from. Hmmm?" I asked, watching him carefully.

Brennan looked at me, and then looked away. Dismissing me, even though I'd just hurt him with the magic of the dragons, even though I was draining him.

It was taking longer than I'd thought, because in spite of being stuck in the Goblin Realm all these years, Brennan had a great deal more magic than I'd thought he would. He was supposed to be strong, as the Goblin King, but I'd always thought my parents put that rumor about to make him feel better about a life confined to the Goblin Realm.

Apparently, some of the rumors were true. He was strong. I forced myself to calm. I had time. No one knew we were here, hidden as we were in this remote castle in the Dragon Realm. Brennan would die at my hands.

"I think, dear brother, that we should start again." I turned away, clasping my hands behind my back. "All these years, we've been unable to share things as brothers should. I believe that should change now." I turned back to him, smiling. "Once I have ended you, I shall pay special attention to your new Queen. See if I can learn just…what…" I let the word trail off suggestively as I raised one eyebrow, "It is about her that…draws you in so."

His face went red, and I could see a muscle in his jaw tighten. But other than another scornful glance at me, he didn't react.

"No? You think she would not be up for the task? Worn out by the Goblin King, perhaps? Well," I busied myself by looking into a pouch at my belt. "That is understandable. She is, after all, only a pathetic human. Still," I glanced back at him with a hopeful smile. "She could be worth some of my time." I sighed. "I am rather busy, you know. You've met my bride, I hear. The lovely and sweet Goblin Princess. The true heir to the Goblin Realm. When you are gone, she and I shall rule together."

I let the magic flow through me, focusing it on Brennan's midsection. Nothing worse than wanting to double over from pain, and being unable to do so. "There is also Ailla, whom you know a bit better. Not as well as you thought, perhaps?"

He didn't respond. Didn't even look at me.

"I had her before she ever came to you. I heard all about you and that pathetic imposter you call brother. She and I laughed as she detailed his struggles. Poor little human, can't stop falling in love with his brother's intended," I mocked. "He's not fit to clean my night chamber," I finished. "Ailla told me it was the easiest thing she'd ever done. He offered up very little resistance. Perhaps he is not as loyal as you think?"

Still no reaction. He *was* stronger than I thought. No matter. I would break him, and I would have his magic.

And then I would kill him.

"What do you mean, he got away?" I took in the room, and Ailla's disheveled appearance. It looked as though she'd been hit in the face. "What is wrong with your face, Ailla?" I asked. I had to struggle to keep from hitting her myself.

She glared at me. "That little upstart hit me!"

"How did she get close enough to put her hands on you?" I asked.

"It wasn't only her! Drake and some mage were with her."

I looked around. "Where is Aine?" The strange girl was helpful when I needed to increase the intensity of my spell work. I didn't know why. When I'd mentioned it to Eilor, he had not given me any answer as to why that might be.

It's why I insisted Ailla bring her along to this sad outpost. There was a reason Eilor kept Aine around him, close to him at all times. I hadn't discovered what it might be, but she was useful, and anything that he wanted was valuable. Even if I didn't know the true value yet.

"What do you want her for?" Ailla's jealousy flared brightly.

"Because she will help me to extend my searching spell, to find the man that you let go," I said cruelly, not caring if my words hurt her. Ailla was fast becoming a nuisance. Her body bored me, her tantrums and anger even more so.

If I wasn't worried that Eilor would cut me out of whatever he was planning, I would have left off with Ailla some time ago. But she'd convinced him that I was central to his plans, and completely supportive of what he wished to accomplish. I wasn't quite sure what those plans were, but again, if he considered them important, so did I. From her retelling, I wasn't sure that he was as convinced as she was. I'd not been able to break things off with Ailla with such uncertainty surrounding my position.

I worried that Ailla hadn't heard from him in a few days. They were normally in contact daily. Things had gone awry ever since Brennan had called off their engagement and shown up with a human girl.

I'd seen her a few times. She was small, pale, and blonde. Both Ailla and Dhysara were tall, and dark-haired. A blonde woman might be an interesting change. An idea began to form—

"It can wait a little, can't it, Cian?" Ailla moved closer to me, her hands drifting down along my body.

I enjoyed the sound of my name on her red, pouting lips. I'd told it to her, in a moment of passion, ignoring the warnings that it might not be the best idea. She'd reacted with the appropriate awe and deference I was due. To hear her crying out my name—my true name—as she lost control at my hands, no matter what I did to her, was worth it.

She knew who her master was. I would soon be master of all the Realms.

Ailla continued. "Brennan is hurt. They will move slowly so as to not hurt him more." Her hands became more insistent, grasping me beneath my clothes. The thought of small, pale hands and a blonde head bent over the same work inflamed me.

"I miss you," she whispered, stopping her endeavors to look up at me and reach for her bodice.

I grabbed her hands, pushing her against the table where Brennan had been. I pulled up her gown, not interested in waiting for her to disrobe. I no longer saw her. Instead, the small blonde woman was before my eyes, little hands trapped in mine, body splayed out beneath me. Tugging, struggling, and trying to get away. Every movement a whispered promise. My breath caught. I'd seen into Brennan's head, seen what he'd experienced with the human.

As Ailla lay back, pulling me to her, I saw only blonde hair strewn across the table and smiled. I entered her roughly, wanting her to fight me, to protest. To bring my vision and the moment closer.

Ailla's cries caused the servants to come to the door. I ignored them as I poured my thoughts, my frustration, and my longing into her, seeing the tears fall like brilliant stones into the blonde hair that filled my vision and nearly took the life from me.

CHAPTER 5

Ailla wasn't speaking to me. I didn't know where Eilor had disappeared to. He wasn't in the Dragon Realm.

After Brennan escaped, and Ailla attempted to distract me, I'd contacted Niles. As Eilor's Court Mage, he would know where the king was.

But Niles claimed he had no knowledge.

The man was lying. I could feel it.

Worse, I could feel that something was awry. Nothing had gone well since I'd gotten the mirror call from Dhysara. I sighed. I'd need to go and see her, as well. She was mooning away in the mirror, wanting me to come home.

As if that little ramshackle hut could ever be a home.

Dhysara was very sweet, and it was most gratifying that she loved me. But she was simple and she no longer cared if she ever regained the Goblin Throne. I couldn't understand it. She was the heir. It was hers, by birth, and by right.

Like me, Brennan had taken it from her.

With Ailla angry, it made the castle uncomfortable. I opened a portal, and went to see Dhysara.

When I arrived, she was in a chair by the window, gazing out. When she saw me, she sprang from the chair.

"Kelan, my love!" She flew into my arms, and wrapped herself around me.

The feeling of contentment that I so rarely felt anymore washed over me. Why did it have to be with Dhysara, who was the most tepid woman I'd ever bedded? Why couldn't it have been with Ailla?

The thought of Brennan's little bride flashed through my mind, and I felt my heartbeat quicken. As Dhysara kissed me, I pictured the human standing on her toes, trying to get closer to me. I closed my eyes, and let the picture become clearer.

Dhysara let me go before I was ready. While I'd never taken any resistance from Ailla, I was careful with Dhysara. She was soft, and gentle, and I did not wish to hurt her. But the thought of the pale human haunted me, and I struggled not to take Dhysara to me, to exorcise the need I felt.

"How are you, my sweet?" I said.

"I have missed you, my love. Are you here to stay with me?"

I put a somber expression on my face. "I am sorry to tell you that no, I am not. I am on a mission for Eilor. He is working to squelch some dissenters that have been giving him trouble. But he doesn't wish to alarm the Court, so he asked me to help him."

Dhysara beamed. "Of course he did. You are far more skilled than any of his mages, Kelan."

Some of my ferocious need calmed under her proud gaze. Dhysara always made me feel…better.

"Have you been harassed any further by the Goblin King?" I asked. I couldn't believe he'd come here—and I wanted to see if she knew he was missing. If she'd heard anything. If he'd come here looking for me.

She shook her head, but she wouldn't look at me. I could feel an air of discomfort from her. That was odd.

I gently lifted her chin. "Dhysara?" I asked. There was something more here.

"Can we not let this go?" She burst out. "I do not care if I ever sit upon the throne! We have a good life, here, Kelan! You and I are happy together. I do not like how restless the Dragon King and his plans make you these days. Tell him no, tell him you are done with his schemes, and let us move our lives forward together!" She raised her hands and held my face within them.

In her eyes I could see love, and acceptance. Not even Nanny had looked at me the way that Dhysara did.

"What do you mean, his schemes?" I said, caught suddenly by her words.

"I do not know what he plans, but I know Ailla, and she cannot keep a secret. She's boasted of his plans, even after she was put aside by the Goblin King. She doesn't seem to think that anything amiss has occurred. Who will have her now?" Dhysara sniffed. "But she says her father will make everything as it should be." She pulled me closer to her.

"I have lived in the Dragon Realm almost as long as you have, Kelan. You know as well as I do that Eilor is always immersed in a scheme."

I couldn't keep looking at her honest, trusting eyes. They said too much, and saw even more.

"My love," I said, trying not to yell at her. "You know that we owe him all. He saved me and my mother," the lie fell easily from my lips, "And he sheltered you and yours. I cannot refuse him. I do not want the Realm to fall into dissension, or worse, rebellion. I must help him."

"Stay with me for a time," she begged. "I love you, and I am lonely without you."

I bent down, letting my head rest on her neck, inhaling her sweet smell. There was something different about the way she smelled, but it wasn't unpleasant. She was warm and I felt comforted with her arms around me.

She led me to the small bedroom off of the main room and we carefully, slowly undressed. Her body was warmer than I remembered, and more softly rounded. Perhaps it was because she was in such stark contrast to Ailla, who was all nails and teeth and blood and pain.

At the memory of my last encounter when the pale blonde waif settled over Ailla's features, I felt my blood quicken, and my heart began to race.

I turned to Dhysara with greater need than I'd had in some time, and by the time she, at least, was fully sated, both of us were sweating and disheveled.

But still, my desire to bend the human to my will hummed through me. I had to get rid of Brennan. And my parents. Then I would hold control over all the Realms, and everything that I wanted, everything I deserved, would be open to me. I would be able to remove the blonde hair and pale face from my memory once and for all.

Brennan. I had to get rid of Brennan. Brennan who had cheated me, tried to kill me, usurped my place in our family, and then outright replaced me. Brennan who was the keeper of the pale blonde woman, who infected me like a rash.

Why was Dhysara so weak that she wouldn't see that Brennan needed to die? With him gone, she could have the life she'd always lived. Not this sad and dingy dwelling with its peeling walls and moldering odor. She deserved better. I deserved better.

It always, always came back to Brennan. He had to die.

Unless he died, I could never live as I should.

Dhysara reached for me, stroking my face. She never hesitated as her fingers brushed across my scar. Unlike many of the fae, my scar didn't bother her. It was almost as though she didn't see it at all.

"I miss this time with you, Kelan. Will you hurry back? Take care of Eilor's needs, and come back to me? Then we may shut out the world, and be only the two of us."

How could she not see? How could she not see that until Brennan died, I would never be truly alive? Until my parents and Brennan paid for all they had done, I was incomplete and wanting? Why did no one, not even Dhysara, see that?

Why didn't she care that Brennan had taken all from her as well? Even though she knew me only as Kelan, she knew that I had lived with slights and injuries while in the Dragon Court. It had been bold of me to ask for her hand. In order to be seen as good enough to wed the Goblin Princess, I needed to strike out, lift myself up. Even though I knew I should be the Fae King, I also knew I needed to be the fae man that Dhysara deserved. Helping her to regain her throne was part of that.

And she was willing to throw it all away. Did she love me so little?

I shrugged from beneath her soft touch, rising from the bed. I found my clothing where it had dropped and began to dress.

"I am sorry, my love," I said, smiling and hoping to keep the flames within from burning me to cinders. "I must return. I only had a short time, but I thought it would be good to sneak away to see you."

She rose from the bedclothes, beautiful and naked. She embraced me, and helped me to dress. Then she wrapped herself around me, kissing me deeply, and tenderly. The feel of her naked form against the leather clothing was intoxicating.

The warm scent from her rose up like mist on the water, and for a moment, I was tempted. How easy it would be to stay here, let her tend to me and love me.

But if I gave in, Brennan would win.

He'd been winning my entire life. He would not win this.

I kissed her once more, and then I left the bedroom.

After a moment, she followed, wrapped in a robe. "Come back to me soon, my love," she said.

"I will. I shall lay the world at your feet, my sweet princess," I said.

"I don't want the world. I already have it right here," she stepped into my arms, which rose up to embrace her almost of their own accord.

I eased from her, casting a portal as I did so. Dhysara crossed her arms, watching me silently. I could feel the weight of her words, spoken and unspoken, in her gaze.

When I made to step into the portal, I turned to look at her again.

"I love you," she said.

"I love you," I answered.

I stepped through, and was back in the outpost. In the wrecked room that might be the ruin of all my plans.

Now I needed to go and find Ailla, and take the next step. Brennan, due to her, had escaped. I was certain that my parents knew about me by this time. I cursed Dhysara for distracting me. I could have gotten to them first—put that aspect of the plan into motion. But she had to carry on about her needs.

This was why Ailla was so vital. She didn't hesitate, but charged into action. I needed to smooth things over with her, and then we would leave.

The Fae King was going to die today. Once he did, so would the rest of his family.

And then I would be complete. All those who hurt me would be gone.

I could begin to live once more.

CHAPTER 6

$\mathcal{I}$ watched around me as the remnants of those I considered family stood motionless, poised to kill me. My mother lay on the floor. Somehow, that little mongrel Aine was there, bent over her, and trying to help her. Stupid girl.

I'd have no choice but to kill Nerida, but not immediately. She had expressed her sorrow, and it seemed genuine. I would need to leave her alive after the others were gone, to speak with her more.

I watched Aine for a moment. I wondered how she'd come to be here, when she was supposed to be in the castle in the Dragon Realm, doing as she was bid. I would need to investigate that once this was done.

I found that in spite of what I'd thought, I was not immune to seeing these people. They were—had been— my family. But when I looked at their faces, all of them wore the expression of murder. After more than six hundred years

Ailla and I were protected by the spell I'd cast. None of

them could get close to us, either by magic or sword. This was the end.

Jharak said something, and I replied, not paying attention.

Then he spoke again. "So you admit, you are my son?" asked Jharak.

"I admit that at one point, I was your son," I answered, feeling tired. "I am your son no longer. However, I will be what I should have always been. After tonight, I will be the Fae King. There's nothing you can do to stop it."

They were closing in, thinking that they had a chance. They had no idea of what I was capable of. Drake, a man who looked to be a mage, Jharak, and *her*. The pale, blonde wife of my brother. She stared at me with a fierceness that thrilled me.

Along with Nerida, she would need to live a bit longer. I needed to see if her skin was as pale as my thoughts painted her. How it would redden to the touch. And then I needed to excise her from my thoughts.

Ailla would not be happy. She harbored a deep grudge against the human. Not only for her face, but apparently, for marrying my brother. But she would tolerate it, because I told her to.

And that would be the end of it. I would be able to go on without seeing the blonde hair floating before me.

I opened my mouth but my words were cut off by the opening of a portal.

I knew that portal.

What was *she* doing *here*?

Everyone spoke at once, and it was confusing to sort through the babble. Then, in a moment of clarity, I heard only Dhysara.

"You're going to have a child?" I asked slowly, unsure if I'd heard right.

Dhysara smiled, love radiating from her. "We're going to have a child, Kelan."

I felt the warmth she always brought.

Ailla looked at me, her expression unreadable, and then turned and practically flew towards Dhysara. "His name is Cian! Cian, you stupid brood mare!"

I grabbed her as she made for Dhysara. My wife, the mother of my child. Ailla was moving so fast, and I pulled on her so hard, she fell backward onto the floor.

"Don't!" I said to Ailla, glaring at her where she lay on the ground. "Don't move."

Not taking her eyes off me, Ailla gave a little nod, but then immediately turned and glared at Dhysara.

Dhysara smiled at me. "Thank you, my love."

"Dhysara, stay where you are. This could get dangerous." I smiled at her. When this was over—

I returned my attention to Jharak. "Now, Father, it's time for you to make right has been wrong for so long."

"What is it you think I need to make right?" Jharak asked.

"You will step down, and proclaim me the Fae King. You will also bestow upon me the powers of the Goblin King."

The looks of surprise they all had at my words nearly made me laugh. "You think I didn't know? Nanny Margot and Eilor told me all about it. I know exactly why you let me go, why you let me die."

"I can't give you what is not mine to give," Jharak said. "The powers of the Goblin King come to the one who is chosen, and I am not one who does the choosing."

I would not be denied. I had not worked as I had, for all these years for him—for them—to deny me now. I darted forward and grabbed Nerida, who had finally gotten up. I pulled her to me, holding a stone close to her. "You will do as I say, or she dies!"

"Cian!" Ailla cried, from where she still sat on the floor.

"My love, please don't do this!" Dhysara pleaded. I looked at her, and then looked away. I could see the pain in her eyes, the knowledge that I would not be coming back to her. My child…

I briefly caught a glimpse of my father's eyes. He was gathering the energy in the room to—

Then I saw her. The golden woman, hair floating around her, walking towards me. She moved closer and closer, a glow surrounding her as though she were of the sun itself.

I watched as she made her way to me. Her hands were out, and it nearly hurt my eyes to see her. She was beautiful, glorious, and she kept coming towards me. Once she reached me, it would be all that I had envisioned. She would be mine. Dysara, Ailla—they were nothing. This woman—she was fit for a King. For me.

I think others may have tried to stop her, but she would not be denied. She was coming to me, just as I had seen, just as I hoped—

She put her pale, beautiful hands before me, and spoke—

The light became so bright, I had to close my eyes.

CHAPTER 7

*B*rennan stood with his father and brother. Together, they watched as Taranath sank the bodies of Cian and Ailla beneath the ground.

There would be no memory left of these two. There would no place for anyone to remember or mourn them.

Given that their aim had been the destruction of all the Realms, it was fitting.

"Goodbye, brother." He looked down at the body of Cian, wrapped in a shroud, as it disappeared. Cian should have died long ago, not been taken to be warped and molded by Eilor.

Eilor.

They had to find him. He was the evil root from which all the horror sprang.

He glanced over at Jharak. His father's expression was inscrutable. Brennan didn't envy him, although Jharak had done what he needed to. No one wanted to bury a child.

Drake, too, was hard to read.

Together, they stood watching until there was no evidence of any disturbance in the ground.

It was done.

"Let's go," Drake said quietly. "We have a king to catch."

THE ACCIDENTAL TRAVELER

A Realm Companion Story
Tale #7

To My Everything Outlander Ladies –
Seeking standing stones since 1992

AUTHOR'S NOTE

This is a work of fiction, obviously. But the Clan MacIain, who were a sept of the Clan MacDonald, were very much real. As a named clan, they existed in western Scotland, in the areas I mention in the story. The MacIain's' stronghold was also Mingary Castle, as it is referred to now, (originally known as Mingarry Castle, and Caisteal Mhìogharraidh in Gaelic) which has been restored and looks so lovely it nearly makes your teeth ache with longing to visit. The MacIains lost Mingary in the early seventeenth century due to, as Wikipedia puts it, "the duplicity of Clan Campbell." If you read the history around this, that phrase doesn't do the "duplicity" justice.

I have taken liberties with the timeline, and put my MacIains/MacDonalds at Mingary Castle in the early eighteenth century, because I think if I went with historical accuracy, Eleanor couldn't have understood Roderick. I might be wrong, but four-hundred years felt a bit of a stretch.

You will also see various spellings of MacIain. I am

going with the current spelling that is used on the <u>Clan</u> website.

This story came about because in researching something else, I saw pictures of the beginning of the restoration of Mingary. It is so beautiful that I kept stalking the site and decided I had to write a story about it. As I researched the area, I was saddened to find that the Clan MacIain was considered by some to be a disappeared clan, meaning they'd lost their lands, and combined with other clans. (Iain MacIain would strongly disagree.)

I wanted to right that loss, even if only in fiction.

So for my historical inaccuracy, please forgive me. Any MacIains or MacDonalds of Ardnamurchan, forgive me as well.

And yes, there is a reason this is part of The Realm series.

Lisa

PROLOGUE

*S*ettled into the couch, hoping not to be disturbed. The kids were at school, my husband at work. The peace and quiet of the house allowed everything but my thoughts to calm.

How could they? For the past week, everything had been upside down. Not in a good way either.

Damn that pile of molding stones and any and all flashing portals straight to hell. While I was at it, damn Roderick MacIain MacDonald with them. Had they—and he—let me be, I could have come back, and none of this would have happened. My life wouldn't have gone to utter hell.

It's one thing to ruin your own life. But when you stand and have to watch others ruin it, it's hard not to be bitter.

I was one big cup of bitter at the moment.

My thoughts went back to seven months ago. It had been me who insisted we go to Scotland. It sounded wonderful. And it was. Gorgeous and breathtaking, it made me see why people waxed poetic over the place.

It had also shattered my life as I knew it.

CHAPTER 1

*S*even Months Earlier

I strolled down the country lane, enjoying the silence. Family vacations were wonderful, but it was nice to have some time alone. Marcus and the children had gone off on a trip to Skye. I had begged off with a headache. I was well-known for getting headaches that came with pressure changes, and as we were rather high altitude-wise in comparison to our home, it was seen as legitimate. Since they'd be gone overnight, they didn't want me to be ill the entire day. I understood, and I'd stayed behind. It wasn't a hardship, I thought with a grin. Mingary Castle, the hotel where we were staying, was breathtaking. While Marcus had grumbled at bit at the cost, it was worth every cent. To wake in the morning and walk out and look over the sea… there was nothing like it.

I really wanted a bit of down time. Marcus and the kids liked to be on the go. After everyone had left, I'd read for a while, had a second breakfast, feeling very much like one of the hobbits, and then decided I would go out and enjoy the sunshine. They had really picked a nice day for their trip. I was glad for them.

I was also glad for me. The day warmed me as I followed the worn track of the lane. There were fences along one side of the lane, and in the distance, I could see sheep, and some larger brown shapes that I knew were Highland cattle. Large horns, long stringy hair. This was beautiful countryside, and I was so glad that we were here.

There were birds somewhere in the distance, but they weren't really close to me. It added to the silence of the day, in spite of how large and welcoming it was. I felt the sun, and breathed in the smell of grass. Even the faint tang underneath of sheep and cattle didn't bother me. Normally, such smells make me crazy. Ever since I'd had my children, my sense of smell was extremely sensitive and I could smell things that many people couldn't. I continued on, stretching my arms even though my hands stayed in pockets. There was a bit of chill in the air. I hope that Marcus remembered sweaters for himself and the kids. They'd be grumpy when they got home if not. That would not be a fun ending for anyone's day. As I walked, I set concerns about the others aside. They'd manage. It was so lovely here. I kept looking around, my head going from side to side as I soaked in the atmosphere.

I stopped, looking off to the pastures to my left, and then continued on. I took two, maybe three steps. I tripped over something hard and sharp that hurt my foot even through my hiking shoes. I didn't realize there were such large stones in the path.

As I fell forward, I saw a flash, a—a circle of light? Where had that come from?

I could hear a voice—a man's voice-- "Stupid woman, move out of the way!" Then words I didn't understand.

Before I had time to look more closely, or see who was

talking, I felt a sharp pain, first in my side, and then my face. All I could see were stars. Everything went dark.

When I opened my eyes, my face was pressed against ground. I must have been there for a while, because I could feel the indentation of small rocks and gravel in my cheeks. I pushed myself up slowly, leaning on my elbow, brushing the dirt and grit off me that I could reach. I made to get up, but stopped when I looked in front of me. A pair of black boots, oddly held together by what looked like partially tanned leather straps coming up to the very knobby, hairy knees, stood right in front of me. I lifted my eyes a little bit further, and I saw – was that? Oh, no. Oh, *no*. Oh my God.

It couldn't be—but it was. I had two kids. I knew what the lower half of a man looked like. Even from this angle. I looked back down. I'm not sure this could get any more embarrassing.

This *was* Scotland, after all. It made sense that the locals would go around in kilts. It was the national dress, and here in the countryside, I noticed that people were a mix in what they wore. Most wore normal everyday clothes — jeans, sweaters, and the like – but some of the older folk, and a few of the younger folk, really enjoyed kilts. I thought they were marvelous looking, so I understood. This angle however--not so wonderful. I belatedly remembered what Scottish men were said to wear beneath their kilts. Now I could say that in my case, I'd found it to be true. I hoped that I wasn't as red as a tomato but the heat in my cheeks suggested otherwise.

I took a few deep breaths. Feeling like I had greater control over myself, I looked up again at the man, hoping to cover my gaffe with a smile. I hadn't *meant* to look up his kilt. I was going to pretend that I hadn't seen what I'd just seen.

"I'm sorry, I seem to have taken a fall. Am I on your land? Have I been here long? If you give me a moment, I'll be on my way." I brushed at myself again, feeling uncomfortable with the intensity of his gaze.

Well," his voice was deep, almost rough. He spoke slowly, as though afraid to let too many words out. "That I do not know, Mistress. What time was it when you fell?"

There was a hint of something in question, but I couldn't tell exactly what it was. Sarcasm? He sounded educated, although I could hear the distinct dialect that we heard as we traveled all over the region. He didn't sound exactly like the men I've been hearing is in the various places we stopped. *Don't assume the worst, Eleanor*, I told myself. You need to assume the best. I smiled once more. Try again.

"Well, I'm not sure myself. I was taking a walk when I tripped over the stones. Could I hire you to help me back to the village, or at least my hotel? I don't know that I'm all that steady." I gestured behind me where I thought they— the stones, the castle, the little village in the distance —were.

He interrupted me. "Village? Hotel? Mistress, do you jest with me?" He gestured around him, and the tone of his voice was definitely sarcastic.

"The village that's all around us—" I got to my feet and looked around. What I saw startled me into silence. The day was no longer sunny. It was rather grey and overcast. Clouds scudded across the sky, and there was more wind than there been all morning. The hint of chill I'd felt earlier had matured into cold. It felt as though I'd fallen into a different day. I couldn't see any buildings in the distance. Normally the homes in Kilchoan shone brightly with their white walls.

The man in front of me stood with his hands on his

hips, and looked down. I noticed that he hadn't offered me a hand as I got up--or to help me in any fashion. If anything, he was treating me like a criminal. Someone who must've done something wrong, he just didn't know what it was. But he would find out. It made me feel distinctly uncomfortable.

"Mistress, are you in some distress?"

"I don't know. I do need to get back to the hotel, as my husband and children will be back soon." I didn't know what time it was, but with the way the day had changed— surely I hadn't been out overnight? I didn't think so, but I wasn't telling this kilt-wearing man that my family wasn't around.

His eyebrows went up almost to his hairline. "What hotel, Mistress? Where is it you say your family is lodged?"

"The hotel right there!" I threw up my hands in exasperation. I could see the castle in the distance—I looked again. It looked...different.

He studied me, his eyes raking me up and down in what I could only describe as an inquisitive gaze. It was so naked, so... stark. I felt exposed. Again, I felt as though I'd done something wrong. Maybe it was just him. He had that sort of judicial air about him.

"Mistress, there is no village. A collection of crofts, yes. Certainly no lodgings where one might stay with family. There is only my home, which, while a busy place, does not qualify as a town." He still spoke slowly, as to a child. Probably a good thing. His accent was very pronounced.

"What do you mean, there is no village?" I was getting angry. He was just playing with me. Some sort of prank for the stupid American tourists. "I just walked from there! Now if you don't mind, I need to get back." Deciding he wasn't deserving of any more effort on my part. I turned away from him, intending to stalk away with my right-eousness intact.

He stopped my indignant exit merely by stepping in front of me, and leaned down so that his face was close to mine.

I blinked. His features were strong, his teeth were yellow, and his breath — obviously he'd been eating onions at some point. Like, some point in the last year, because the onion was strong all over him. I felt I could even smell it in the—was that a fur? The cape or whatever it was that he wore. He was not ugly, but not entirely handsome. He was, I don't know. He reminded me of a soldier, a soldier who had long been at war. Tough and grizzled. Too much life to be handsome? The odd thought went through my head.

"Mistress, there are none on my lands that move about without my permission. I do not know you, nor do I recall giving you, or this supposed husband and children of yours, permission to take any lodgings here. There is no village, no inn. So I am left to assume that you are lying to me." He glared at me, and the sense of being guilty of something fell over me once more.

He continued, "That also leads me to ask why a young woman such as yourself is out all alone. It makes no sense, and I will have the sense of it. You shall come back to the castle with me, and we'll see what is to be done with you." Without waiting for an answer, he took one of my arms. He turned in the direction that I thought I'd been heading and begin to march away, nearly dragging me along with it.

"Hey, what do you think you're doing? Stop that! Let me go!" I struggled against arm was holding mine, I couldn't get away. His grip only tightened as he kept walking.

"Mistress, I've made myself plain. There's no more discussion to be had. We return to Mingary."

What? Mingary? I would have remembered seeing this guy around the place. He was definitely not a guest, and certainly not the proprietor of the upscale property.

I was running to keep up with him as he towed me along. "Stop that! Stop that!" I yanked on the arm he had a hold of but all it did was hurt my shoulder. "What are you? Are you some kind of kidnapper? Let me go!"

He looked down at me again, and now he was angry. I could see it in the furrowing of his brow, the fire in his eyes. This was a guy with a temper.

That was interesting. Most people generally try to hide their short fuses. At least pretend to manage them. That expression — it took me back quite a bit. It was scary. He was mad, pissed even, and he didn't care who saw it. He was secure enough in himself, what was his life was to let his anger shine through with no check.

My gut told me it was time to be very scared.

CHAPTER 2

Three Months Later

In between the time that I had arrived Mingary, and the present, I asked daily as to whether my husband had written, and every day, MacDonald said, *No, he had not.* Now, having gotten to know the castle and the man who ran it a little better, I had a thought as to why he kept telling me no.

I didn't think that he was dishonest. MacDonald had a wicked temper, and he wasn't afraid to show it, something I'd noticed the first time I'd met him. Had he received word from anyone about me, he would have told me. He had a strong sense of honor.

Even thought I knew good and well he wouldn't hear a thing, I needed to keep up the pretense. It took me a while to see it but I started to get the impression that he was happy no word had come for me.

Sadly, he was the only one in the castle who felt that way. He had three daughters, all married to lesser men than he was, and they were very upset at his attentions to me. They saw what was happening before I did.

I kept up my manners, which weren't as hard to manage as they'd been in the beginning. Because I didn't give him any trouble, when I asked to be allowed to walk the lane where I'd fell, he let me. He had me followed of course. I existed in that strange place somewhere between a guest of the house, and a prisoner.

And last night, he'd been quite pleasant, and complimentary. His daughters all glowered, their faces beacons of anger in the darkened hall. It was coming. He was going to propose something permanent for me. The kids were pissed, and didn't like it. I wasn't sure what it would be, but he'd made efforts to be a lot nicer in the past week, and that wasn't his normal behavior. I knew something was up.

The feeling of being on the edge of throwing up returned. It hadn't been as present recently, but the thought of being sent somewhere, or told what to do scared the daylights out of me. I told myself to buck up— these people respected strength and courage. I'd have to find some.

Since there was no way I was bringing up all the shifts I'd noticed, I planned to go on my walk as normal after breakfast. Maybe some food would settle my nerves. Or make it easier to puke—but I pushed that thought away.

I took care getting dressed and made my way to the hall. Once I made it there, I pretended I didn't notice all the undercurrents swirling around. The past week had been different. I was English, in spite of my insistence that I was an American. Since MacDonald—recently he'd asked me to call him Roderick, which seemed a big deal— began treating me more kindly, I'd seen a change in the rest of the inhabitants of the castle.

It was interesting – the people here trusted Roderick absolutely. Everything that he did was good. His temper, the fact that he was prone to anger—it didn't matter. Over the past week, outside of his immediate family, everyone I'd come across had taken the time to tell me what a good man he was. As though my opinion of him mattered, when two weeks ago, there were remarks made in Gaelic as I passed.

This only increased my unease as to what plans might be.

This morning, I sat quietly, eating my porridge. The only thing you got here with porridge was salt. I desperately missed cream and sugar and butter. Maybe even some honey. But that wasn't the norm here. So I took the salt offered, and leaned over my bowl, eating my porridge in silence. I'd done this every day for the last three months. Normally, Roderick sat next to me, equally silent. He was of the belief, I'd learned, that if you had nothing to say, it was better to remain silent. I didn't agree—but this wasn't my house, and no one here would ever side with me against the MacDonald.

So I kept my mouth shut, and ate quietly, making no noise or eye contact.

This morning, however, he had something to say. I could feel it coming. My suspicions from last night were right.

Finally, when he finished his porridge, he turned to me.

"Mistress Eleanor, I have made a decision."

Oh?" I said. I wasn't going to make this easy. It was bad enough he felt he had the right to say what I would or wouldn't do.

"It has been three months, Mistress. Your husband is not searching for you. I sent out letters far and wide. No one has come forth to claim you. Therefore, I can only assume that you lied to me." He stopped, letting everyone around us have time to digest what he'd said.

Thanks, guy. You're a peach. I looked up finally, as

though we were doing nothing more than discussing the weather. "Is that is your deduction?"

He inhaled deeply, trying to keep himself from getting annoyed. I hid my smile. Lord on all high he might be, but he was so easy to set off.

"Yes, that is my deduction," he stressed the last word.

I doubted any of the faithful heard the sarcasm.

He continued, "In spite of your words, and my efforts, it is apparent to me that you are alone in the world. You have no family, no one to care for you."

I held up a hand at that moment. "I do have a solution to this—"

He spoke as though I had said nothing. "You shall marry me, Mistress. That way, you share my name, my clan, my protection. You will be safe."

"What?" I know my mouth fell open. I know it wasn't the best look. But of all the things I'd been thinking, this was the last one I'd expected.

"I can't marry you," I said.

Roderick stood, and addressed the hall. "The Mistress Eleanor and I shall be married in three days' time! We shall celebrate together, as a clan!" He nodded at the room, and then sat back down, taking a long drink from his tankard. It was obvious that he was satisfied with this days work.

After a moment, the hall exploded into conversation. I didn't get the impression that the people here were all that surprised. That explained the increased friendliness, and the extolling of the laird's virtues the past week. I risked at glance at Roderick's daughters, and son-in-laws. They were livid. I turned from them. That was their problem. I had bigger concerns.

"I will not marry you!" I hissed at him. "I can't! I'm already married, and I don't want to marry a guy who kidnapped me! I shall not marry you." I sat back in my chair, clenching my teeth.

"At this moment, Mistress, your wish no longer matters. You've taken much of my hospitality. It's the only right thing to do, for the sake of modesty and your soul." His mouth quirked. Even though we attended Mass every Sunday, I knew without having to be told that Roderick had a rather cynical view of the church. "I cannot have an unmarried woman here for as long as you've been here without the bonds of matrimony. I will not allow my reputation to be sullied. Or yours," he added, although clearly that was an afterthought.

I could be offended, but I wasn't. "My reputation doesn't matter. And if you just let me go, yours will sustain no further damage," I lowered my voice to allow a little pleading come into it.

Until this moment, he had not looked at me even as he sat next to me. But now, he turned his head to look at me, the tanker halfway towards his mouth. He grinned a feral grin. The grin of a triumphant wild animal. "No, Mistress. That is not how we see it all. My reputation will be beyond repair. It nearly is now. The only way out of this for you is to marry me. It will do you no good to argue. And do not think you can get away from me. My household will keep you within their sight at all times. It is time to accept facts, Mistress. Three days hence, we shall be joined as man and wife." Apparently, he felt the conversation was done, because he turned back to watch the people in the hall, taking a swallow from his tankard.

The smug satisfaction that radiated off him was pervasive, like the smell when you hit a skunk with your car. It made me want to brain him with my bowl. The worse part was, he was right. In the three months that I've been here, I've learned everything that he said was right.

Even though lately, people had been singing his praises to me, I couldn't miss the comments made in Gaelic as I moved around the castle. It was one of the reasons I took longer walks each day. I couldn't stand the judgement. So...Roderick was right. Damn him. But if he'd just let me go, this could all disappear. I didn't understand why he wouldn't leave me be and let me find my own way home.

While I was considering this, I thought of my kids. Like I did every single day. What were they doing? How were they doing? My poor kiddos. All I wanted was to get back to them, and Marcus, and forget this ever happened.

But it looked as though I wasn't going to get that. Since I had the freedom to walk, I nearly wore my own path in the place where I'd tripped into that light thing. I hadn't seen it again. And I was looking. I looked so hard I thought my eyes were going to fall out of my head. So even if Roderick let me go...where would I go?

I sighed. It seemed I didn't have any real choices here. I turned from him, and watched the crowd. People looked like they were happy for Roderick, but that could also be the extra ale that was being served. Well, other than his kids. I took a drink from my cup. I'd have to make sure I didn't end up with poison in my porridge, given the expressions on their faces.

True to his word, three days later, Roderick and I were married. I moved through the motions of the wedding in a state of shock. This wasn't me. This wasn't happening.

Roderick didn't notice. He threw a huge party, and introduced me to a lot of the neighbors. Not that I could remember any of them. Roderick was happier than I'd seen him, boisterous and loud. He kept his arm around me the entire time, guiding me through this nightmare.

Can't have the little woman falling down and passing

out, now can we? I thought bitterly. That was all I wanted
to do, and he wouldn't even let me do that.

Bastard.

Finally it was time to head up to bed. Ribald laughter
and jokes accompanied us. As he closed the door to his
room behind us, the reality of what was about to happen
hit me, and I could feel my stomach churn. I'd put off
everything around me all day.

But I couldn't any longer.

Oh, God. I'd have to sleep with him.

I wasn't ready—didn't want—any of this. How had I
come to this? The panic lapped at my feet in waves, a
prelude to a tsunami of fear. My arms were starting to
shake. I thought I might fall down.

Oh, God.

Roderick went to the fire and began stripping.
"Eleanor, you'll need to come to bed with me, but you've
nothing to fear."

"What?" I asked. I couldn't think straight. My hands
were cold, and I wrapped my arms around myself, trying
to stop the shaking. My thoughts were splintering off in a
million different directions. This man held my life in his
hands—right down to my physical person. Reluctantly, I
forced myself to listen to him.

"I have no intention of touching you unless you ask. I
know that I am seen as a hard man, but I don't enjoy
bedding women who don't want me. So if you please,
you'll come to bed, and you'll smile and blush when asked
about our wedding night. Should we not consummate this
marriage, it will not be seen as valid. I wish for you to be
protected."

"You're…asking me to lie?" I managed. Not sure that
was the important point, but it was what I grasped.

He sighed, sounding irritated. "Yes. For both our sakes.

You are now the Lady of Mingary. That offers you far greater protection than your former place as an unknown, possibly mad widow."

"Is that what people thought of me?" I was indignant. I'd been nothing but polite to everyone here!

He nodded. "You're not like the women here. You don't talk much, but you're different. Now, you're my lady, and that will quiet any talk."

Apparently the conversation was over. He headed for bed in only his nightshirt. I looked around the room, and saw that I had a nightshirt as well, far nicer than the clothes I'd been wearing. I guess this was part of being the Lady of Mingary.

Keeping my back to the bed, I stripped down and pulled on the nightshirt as fast as possible. Was this a trick? Did he really want to protect me? My hands trembled.

There was only one way to find out. If I ran screaming from the room, that wouldn't help me at all. Taking a breath, inhaling it all the way down to my toes, I turned around.

Roderick was a lump in the bed under the blankets. He didn't speak, or stir.

Cautiously, I walked to the bed. Still careful, I crawled into bed, noting that the sheets were finer than those I'd been sleeping on, and I felt him move as I did so. I tensed, waiting to see what he would do. He reached for my hand, and took it.

"Don't worry, Eleanor. I'll help you. It's all going to be fine." Then he squeezed my hand for a moment, and let go. He turned over, putting his back to me, and didn't speak again.

As the fire died down, and the shadows grew longer, I laid there, eyes wide open, thinking about all that he'd said. This was not what I'd expected. I'd spent a night in my former rooms crying about the fact that I was going to have to sleep with a man who wasn't my husband, my choice, or my anything.

This was the nicest I'd ever seen him.

As the night grew silent around us, the sounds of the celebration below in the hall faded. I felt the muscles in my back relax from the tense position I'd been in the past three days.

For a forced marriage, it wasn't the worst wedding night possible. I hoped that he was right – that it would all be fine.

CHAPTER 3

To my surprise, Roderick was right. Things were better.

He whispered to me when I encountered things in daily life that were part of being a lady of the house and it made my life a hell of a lot easier.

Every night when we went to bed, I tensed, waiting for the other shoe to drop and for him to demand his marital rights. He didn't. Gradually, I started to be able to sleep.

One thing I realized was how isolated I was before. Now that I was married to the Laird, the woman were different. They made allowances for the fact that I didn't speak Gaelic, repeating themselves in English when I asked questions. The fact that Roderick was with me more often than not might have had something to do with it.

But he was seen as being happy to be married, and in their normal way, the people of Mingary were happy for their leader. He excused himself from a lot of his daily tasks initially to be with me, telling people, "I cannot stay away from her!" and accompanied that whopper with a bawdy laugh. People bought it.

The combination of my willingness to learn and Roderick's hovering made a difference. Especially when he would take me on his tasks, keep me with him as well.

After three—almost four—months, the women were a lot friendlier, and the men respectful. It wasn't the worst life, but I missed my children terribly. I dreamed of them nightly. I sometimes woke with tears on my cheeks. Roderick didn't say anything even though I knew he saw the dried tears in the morning.

One thing that I was noticing was that I didn't miss Marcus as much as I thought I ought to.

That troubled me and filled me with guilt. Trying to hold onto my life before and the one I was forced to live now was wearing. I tried not to dwell, because in all fairness, Roderick was making a lot of effort for me. *More than Marcus had made for me in a long time*, a traitorous voice whispered to me. When I got back—I refused to think otherwise—my feelings, or lack thereof, towards Marcus would need to be addressed.

Roderick continued to not force me, or touch me in any way when we were alone. In public, he confined himself to putting an arm around my waist, or tucking my arm into his.

I woke one night in a panic to find that his arms were around me, and him snoring quietly in my ear. His body felt foreign to me, and I didn't like it. I lay stiffly, and fell back to sleep some time later. The next morning, he was on his side of the bed, and he didn't say anything. It pissed me off something fierce but I knew how women were treated as wives here, and I was grateful that he didn't push matters. It made me even angrier that I had to be be grateful he didn't force himself on me. I also wondered if I were experiencing some Stockholm syndrome.

In this state of half-acceptance, half-defiance I carried on. Smiled, behaved graciously, and acted appreciative.

But I couldn't give up getting home. I continued my walks. I had a lot more responsibility as the Lady MacDonald of the Clan MacDonald so I had to take several shorter walks rather than the long walk I was used to taking before I married.

And still, no light. No man yelling. Nothing.

Damn it. I did not want to die here away from my children.

Things continued on. My life was not horrible, but there were so many holes for me that it wasn't happy, either. It was harder for me in the evening when ale was served with dinner. It made me weepy.

I was fighting tears as we were having dinner one night when everyone in the hall was cheerful, the noise rising up towards the rafters. Roderick was in a good mood, smiling and laughing, and even singing along when one of the people in the hall broke into song.

When the last song faded, he leaned over to me, tankard in hand. I studied him. He looked pleased, as he looked around at all of his clan. One of the things I'd learned about him was how deeply he cared for his people. Despite the fact that he'd kidnapped me, I admired this aspect about him. He was happy that they were happy. The hall was much more pleasant than when I'd first arrived, and I wondered how deep his concerns about reputation went. As I was considering this, he spoke for my ears alone.

"Are you ever going to tell me the truth about yourself?"

I was startled. This was not our normal topic of conversation. It wasn't even in the realm of normal topics of conversation. He never asked me about the truth, other than to tell me he didn't think I was telling the truth about husband

I took a drink of ale to stall a little, and hoped like hell I gave the right answer. "What do you mean?"

He turned away, spoke even as he gazed out across the hall. "When you told me how you came to be here, I thought you were lying. I figured that somehow you were planning or part of something underhanded. I watched you. But you didn't do anything suspicious, or anything that would harm my clan. You don't have any skills that a housewife should have. You have to learn everything, everything that goes into the right of how things are done. You seek help and try to learn. So I ask myself, what is the point? All I can come to is that your life must be as you say."

He stopped and looked around, then back at me, looking at me over the rim of the tankard as he drank. "It must also be a fairly easy life, one where you don't do a lot of work. One where your husband provides well. Even as a woman alone, you should have a better sense of how to care for yourself with basic skills. I don't see that you had them when you came here. And your hands—" He picked up my hand not wrapped around the cup. "Your hands, even now, are soft. Not worn from the work a woman needs to do."

Wow. I didn't expect this. I ignored the whole women's work thing, annoying though it was. "Have you been spying on me?" I finally asked. I thought that the days of keeping mad tabs on me were over.

"I am laird here. It's my home, my responsibility. I know everything that goes on here." The quiet fact in his words reminded me that I'd been lulled into a false sense of security in the time since we married.

"And that's what made you believe me? The fact that I don't know how to do laundry?"

He nodded, taking another drink from the tankard as he did so. He wiped his lips, he continued speaking. "Yes. And you have not been afraid of learning. I appreciate that, Eleanor. You're a good woman, and you've been a good wife to me. I've no complaints."

I couldn't help it. I rolled my eyes. "Well, good. I'm so delighted that I've become a good wife." I didn't try to hide the sarcasm. I knew that he was trying to pay me a compliment, but I was still angry about how I'd come to be here. I couldn't get past that. I couldn't get past a lot of things. If I ever—when I got out of here—I'd need some therapy to manage the simmering anger that was with me always these days.

"You should be. It speaks well for you that you to make the effort." He ignored my sarcasm. "I appreciate your efforts Eleanor. Now, I'm asking if you are willing to tell me the truth? Should you choose to do so, I will believe you."

Something in his words struck me. He was being sincere. Nevertheless, I didn't know if he would actually believe me if I told him the truth. What if, after hearing the truth, he had me sent to the stake as a witch? I'd heard from some of the other woman that a number of towns over, there were two woman who had been burned for being witches. To me, it sounded like they were herbalists, or something like that. But there was a lot of superstition and suspicion of the unknown.

One more thing I should be grateful to Roderick for saving me from…but I was mad, and I couldn't let it be.

In addition, I was tired of lying. I was tired of hiding. And I needed him to know if—no when—I found whatever was it brought me here as I walked back and forth on the lane I wouldn't hesitate to leave.

"Roderick, if you wish to know, I shall tell you when we are alone.

His head whipped over to look at me. "So then you have not been telling me the entire truth!" I could see his face redden, like he was getting mad.

So much for the 'I'll believe you' stuff.

"I have told you nothing but the truth. But there's more to it. I have not lied. But I couldn't tell you everything."

He glared, and then yelled something in Gaelic. A serving woman hurried to fill his tankard again.

Great. The moment of kindness was over. Miserably, I sat and watched as he got drunk. The mood in the hall shifted, the people keenly aware that their laird was unhappy. I sat quietly, not speaking to anyone. Finally, I excused myself, hoping he was too drunk to do anything other than fall into bed.

When he came up, I had no idea what time it was, although it was late. He was mumbling to himself, but he didn't address me. So I stayed quiet, on the farthest edge of the bed from him. Thankfully, he didn't make a move toward me. Thank God.

Roderick should have been miserable the next morning, but he was up with the sun. I took my time getting out of bed.

Neither of us spoke. So much for forgetting the conversation via drunkenness. Damn it.

"Wife, we are alone. I require you to tell me the truth."

I didn't like the hard edge to his voice.

I sighed, and turned to face him. Taking a deep breath, I told him the truth. It was hard seeing his face change as I spoke. But he'd asked for it, and I was just too tired to hide it anymore.

I ran from Mingary Castle, the tears rolling down my face. Thankfully, the guards at the gate and the people here were used to me walking. I didn't start to run until I'd left the confines of the castle itself.

Despite what he'd said, when I finished speaking, Roderick took several breaths, his face going red. His eyes showed me he was incensed. I'd felt afraid, for the first time since I'd come here.

He called me a witch, a trick of the devil. He wanted me to get out, and frightened at this change in him, I left. I ran from the room like a rabbit, slamming the door behind me.

After all he'd said last night—I realized that I'd grown to trust him. Not entirely like him, and certainly not love him, but I'd gotten used to him.

And I never expected to have to tell him the truth.

But he been badgering me, going after me the way he did. Needling, his eyes dark and focused on me.

I couldn't stop the tears, which I found odd. I didn't love Roderick. All I wanted was to go home, to see my husband and my children. I didn't want to be here—it wasn't my time.

But my shock over his reaction today—that showed me that I'd gradually become used to my daily life as it was now. Proof positive that people can get used to anything. That scared me.

I clutched the shawl around my head more tightly and pulled up a corner of the shawl to wipe my eyes. The violence of the last half hour had shocked me. I was so tired, and hurt, and worn out—but my legs kept moving, carrying me to the lane I walked every single day.

If ever there was a time for some higher power to intervene, it was now. I couldn't go back to Mingary. Or to Roderick.

In approximately the same area where I had fallen and landed in this wretched time, I had found the rock in the field. It was a rock that had not been there during my time but it was a convenient place to sit. I huddled in my shawl and sat on the rock, trying to figure out what my next move would be.

Was I being foolish? Was it foolish to hope that I would actually get back? Nothing had happened so far. Nothing showed me that I was right. Nothing. Nothing at all!

I felt my anger rise. It was so maddening to have no control over anything! But there was nothing I could do. Well, there was one thing I could do. I wasn't going home tonight.

Where could I go? This was it. I was going to die here. There was no other choice for me. The thought of never seeing my kids again overwhelmed me and I dissolved into great, jagged sobs.

How long I sat there, I didn't know. I must've fallen asleep at some point, because I picked my head up off the stone, looking around for what had startled me.

There it was again—a noise? Something. Something that didn't go with the sounds of the day I'd become accustomed to.

Then, almost directly in front of me, I saw the light. It was the sort of light that shouldn't be here. Even in my own time, this was the sort of light show that one might see at a concert. Green and blue, starting a small circle, floating in midair.

It looked like one of those videos that you saw from the ghost chaser TV shows. The ones where they were always sure something was happening. This kind of evidence— this would've made a lifetime of success for them.

My mouth fell open as the circle about wider and wider. It grew and continue to grow until I could see a shadow within the light. That doesn't sound right, but that's what it was.

My hand flew to my mouth. Was it possible this was something like what had happened to me?

Before I had time to process that idea, a woman stepped from within the light. The light snapped shut behind her. It was like watching the closing of the door.

"What the—?" She looked around, putting her hands on her hips.

"Well, if this isn't just the end. Where am I?"

CHAPTER 4

She was dressed in the kind of clothing that I wore. Well, that I used to wear. Before I landed here. I stood up, letting the shawl fall from my head.

"You're...you're in eighteenth century Scotland," I said. As I spoke, I realized how...*Scottish* I sounded compared to her. She was American, I was sure of it. I couldn't believe she was standing here. And she'd come through the light, like I had!

She let out a little shriek, and jumped backwards, clutching at her chest.

"Oh my goodness! I didn't see you there! Of course, I wasn't expecting to see anyone." She drew herself up, her poise recovered.

I almost laughed. She sounded like a queen.

"Where you from? I mean, what year are you from?" Please let her be from my time! Please, please, please!

"Well, I'm certainly not from the eighteenth century," she said, with a dry tone. "I am from the twenty-first century, and I live in America. Who are you, and why have you not run shrieking from me? Isn't that the normal reaction of people of this time?"

Wow. That was a seriously impressive insta-snotty. But I didn't care. She came through a light. She was my way back.

"I'm not originally from here," I said. "I'm from the same time as you, and I'm an American and I am so glad to see you!" I was trying not to gush, but I was so excited to see someone who might be able to help me get out of here, the words came tumbling out of me. I struggled to my feet with the words falling out of my mouth.

"I was walking down this lane while on holiday with my husband and children, and then I fell. When I woke up, the laird of the castle was standing in front of me. He dragged me back to his castle, and I've been here ever since." I found that my throat tighten as I said the words. So simple. But they didn't even begin to encompass everything that I had endured the last seven months.

"You know how to portal?" She took a few steps towards me, reaching out her hands.

Instinctively, I shrank back a little. Then I stopped, and held my hands up towards her. She took them, pulling me closer. She peered into my face.

"You're not one of the fae," she said. "I recognize you if you were. You're... you're human, aren't you?"

"I am human," I said. "I have no idea what else you're talking about. All I know is that I fell, and somehow, I landed here."

"What is your name, child?" She said, and the snide tone from earlier disappeared altogether. Now she sounded like somebody's grandmother.

I wasn't sure if that reassured me, or made me more on edge.

"My name is Eleanor. Eleanor Hinchcomb. Although now, as I've been forced to marry the man who found me, I'm Eleanor MacDonald. Can you get back to the twenty-first century?" My hands tightened in hers at the thought that I might actually get what I've been looking for all this time.

It didn't seem real. None of this seems real. What were the fae? What was a portal? Why did none of this seem completely Looney Tunes to her?

One thing at a time. If she could get back — then I can go back with her. If she would take me. After that, I gave myself permission to have a mental breakdown. But not right now. Focus, Eleanor!

"My name is Mara. I was trying to get to—well, it doesn't matter. What matters is that the portals are not working. This is not where I should be. That's what matters. Well, that and—" she looked me up and down. "We've got to figure out how to get you out of here as well. That is," her eyebrows went up. "That is, if you want to leave."

My knees gave way, and I staggered to the ground. I lost my grip on one of her hands, but I clung to the other one to keep myself from falling into a heap.

"Do I want to leave? Do I?" I could feel my breath coming in gasps, and my heart was racing as though I'd run a marathon. I could hear ringing in my ears, and nothing seemed real. It felt like at the slightest touch, a breath of wind, I will blow away. Often to the nether somewhere, never to be seen again. I wanted nothing more than to leave, but now that it was here…I couldn't get the words out.

Thankfully, Mara seemed to understand. I wondered if she understood I was on the verge of some sort of break-down. At least, that's what it felt like. I couldn't breathe and my thoughts wouldn't line up or behave enough to make a coherent thought.

She did. "Well, I'll take that as a yes," she said. She squeezed my hand and then let go. I fell over as she did, and then scrabbled on my hands and knees to get up. I didn't want to let her go. I couldn't let the only chance that I had get away from you. "You're not leaving me, are you?" I couldn't even try to disguise the desperation my tone.

She walked away from me a little but she looked around when she heard me speak. "Oh my. Of course not, child. What has happened to you, Eleanor?"

I laughed, a sound with no humor. "What's happened to me? There's not enough time. One thing at a time, Mara. Can you get away from here? Can I come with you?"

"You're ready just to leave?"

"I've been ready to leave for seven months."

She stood, hands on hips, just looking at me. It made me uncomfortable. She was a rather formidable woman, everything about her screaming strength and determination. Finally, as if reaching some decision, she nodded. "Of course, you shall come with me. It will take a little doing, but…" she pursed her lips. "Never mind that. I'll handle it. And I'll help you get back to your family." She stopped speaking then, and begin doing something with her hands.

I scooted a little closer to her, inching almost, because I didn't want to get too far away from her. I could feel that I was on the edge of full-blown hysteria, with only the smallest thing needed to push me over the edge.

After all this time, it was my chance.

While I watched her wave her hands around, and speak in some other language, I thought about something that I'd yelled at Roderick right before I'd run out. I told him, "You don't believe me? Well, one day, I am going to find my way home! I'll leave, vanish, and then you'll know!"

That's when he lost his temper and screamed at me, roaring like a lion. He told me that I could not leave him, that he would not allow it.

How odd and infuriating that I felt a twinge of guilt that I would indeed be leaving.

But I was never meant to be here. And I was never meant to be his. He took me, with no regard for where I was supposed to be, or that I wasn't his to take. Even as he'd been kind, he still took me. Therefore, I was within my rights to look after myself when the chance to go back to where I belong showed up.

I shook my head, aggravated with myself. What did it matter, what Roderick thought? Roderick was not the point here. I was.

Whatever Mara had been doing made a light spark from her hands, and as before, a small circle started to grow. They grew larger than it had when I first saw her, and I realized that my mouth was hanging open.

She glanced over me, smiling. "It is impressive, isn't it?"

I nodded. "What is it?"

"It's a portal, dear. But it's nothing you need to worry about. I would venture to say that you fell through a portal without realizing it. This is one that is stationary, or supposed to be." At my blank look, she laughed a little. "Again, like I said, nothing for you to worry about. Let's just get you home, shall we?"

I gripped her hands, not caring whether I invaded her personal space or not. "Please. Please take me home."

She looked at me for a moment, her expression inscrutable. Then she squeezed my hand in return. "All you need to do a step through it. And then we'll be there."

*O*nce Mara got us back to our time, she took me back to Mingary Castle. Back to the village, and gossip. Back to learning to how to reintegrate into my previous life. I told her the entire thing while I waited for Marcus to make his way back to Scotland. She asked me if I was going to tell him the truth.

"No!" My response was immediate. And then I blushed, because he was supposed to be my husband, and my partner. But like before, when I was at Mingary with Roderick, I found that I wasn't as…sure? Concerned? With Marcus as I had been.

"No one, not even my husband, is going to believe me," I said after a moment, trying to cover my earlier response.

Mara looked at me with a gaze that could only be called piercing, then nodded. "I understand. But I would like you to know that I believe you."

To my surprise, I started to laugh. "I suppose to you it's not such a stretch After all, you travel through a doorway of light, and see nothing wrong with it!"

She joined me in laughing, and I felt better about not telling anyone else the truth. I'd done that once already, and I was pretty sure that I had missed the stake and being burned to death only because Mara rescued me. Roderick's anger after I told him made him into someone I didn't know.

"Well, we better get our story straight, my dear."

That only made me laugh harder. Mara didn't look like someone who would have a story, much less one that she needed to get straight. But after I calmed down, we put together something that would hopefully be believable.

And when I was questioned, I told the story, with much quivering of lip and tear-filled eyes.

Mara backed me up, saying that she found me wandering, and that my assumption was that I was a victim of amnesia because the last thing I remembered was hitting my head. She told the nice constable that had been called that I had told her it was the day after my disappearance.

After a few days, I remembered a big man, bad temper, who loomed over me, but nothing more. I'd been checked over by the local GP, and declared fit for travel. No physical injury.

Which brought me to where was now. Here, at home. Well, what used to be my home? It didn't feel like home anymore. I had my children, which was the only good thing. Marcus, on the other hand, had adjusted to my disappearance just fine.

More than fine, in fact. Once we arrived here, back in my home, Marcus told me how he'd dealt with me vanishing.

He'd had me declared dead.

CHAPTER 5

I was very much alive, and still on the couch cuddled with the dogs when Marcus got home. Going through all that happened sapped any energy I had. Not to mention I now had to untangle the life I'd come back to. I didn't even know where to begin.

He'd come home earlier than the kids every day this week, hoping to…what? Talk to me? I didn't know. What was there to talk about?

I'd been gone for seven months. He'd moved on. Declared me dead. Really, what else was there to say? I didn't say anything because I was afraid. Once words are spoken, given life in the air—they cannot be erased.

"Hey," his voice drifted over my seething thoughts. "How was your day?"

I turned to face him, the biting words fighting to come out and lash him, whip him to shreds. One look at his expression and my hateful words died.

He looked like a guilty sheep, if sheep could look guilty. This wasn't easy on him either. Not that I really wanted to give him any sort of credit for anything at the moment.

I sighed. "I didn't do a damn thing. Not laundry, not the dishes. I pet the dogs. That's it."

He lowered himself into the chair next to the couch, moving carefully. As though I might go off like a bomb.

It wasn't an unfair comparison. Still, it made me angry. What was wrong with the man I'd loved most of my adult life? When had he become so selfish? So weak?

Why hadn't I seen it before? Because Roderick...I stopped myself. Why was I thinking of Roderick when I thought of men in my life? He was not my man, and no longer in my life. He was never supposed to be.

But Marcus was, and he wasn't really in my life anymore, either.

Shit. Just trying to sort this mentally made me tired.

"How about you hang out with the kids today, and I'll take care of dinner?"

I stared at the TV, wishing I'd turned it on before he got home. I'd have something to focus on. I nodded, crossing my arms in front of me.

As carefully as he'd sat, he stood, still moving slowly. "Okay. I'm...I'm going to go see what we have for dinner."

With that, he disappeared from the study, and I heard him go down the stairs to the kitchen. In a moment, I heard the murmur of his voice.

Of course. Calling *her*.

It seemed no time at all before I heard the kids come through the door. They talked with Marcus, voices dropping. Talking about crazy Mom again.

I got up, and went upstairs to tidy up. Whatever else happened, my kids deserved better.

When I came down the stairs, they were all laughing and standing in the kitchen together. My beloved children. Constance, my oldest, turned and her face lit up.

"Mom! I thought you were napping."

"Nope. I decided to get up today." I smiled to show her that I meant no ill with my words.

She came to me and wrapped her arms around me. "I'm glad. I love you, Mom."

I kissed the top of her head. "Love you too, Stanzy."

Dean, the younger of the kids, joined us in the embrace. "It's good to see you up, Mom."

My poor kids. This wasn't the way you wanted your life to go at seventeen and fifteen.

I looked at them, and both had hopeful expressions on their faces.

"It's getting better, guys. I promise."

"Of course it is," Marcus interjected from where he leaned on a counter across the kitchen. "Why don't you guys get going on your homework?"

"Sit with us, Mom?" Dean asked, stepping away but holding onto my hand.

"I'd love to, although you all know a lot more than I do," I said with a small laugh.

Whatever he'd been about to say got lost as the dogs went off right before the doorbell did. How they knew that, I didn't know. But they always let us know when someone was at the door, regardless of whether the doorbell rang.

"I'll get it," Marcus pushed off the counter and hurried through the dining room to the front door. Eager to get away from the potential picture of the happy family, I thought snidely.

I could hear voices, and then Marcus came back into the kitchen.

"Ellie? It's for you." Anger loomed over the question in his words.

"For me? Who is it?" I didn't move.

He shook his head. "I don't know. It's a guy in a kilt, and he says that he has to speak to you."

Ah. Now I understood the reason for the question. And the anger. Scotland was forever changed for us all, as were all things Scottish.

I walked towards the front room, feeling my heartbeat accelerate. I couldn't think about kilts, or…anything associated with them for very long.

I wasn't going to be able to avoid it. A man stood in my formal front room, two men, actually, and Marcus was correct. One of them wore a kilt.

He turned around, and I gasped.

"Ma'am? Are you Eleanor MacKay?" The man in the kilt asked.

"I…I was. MacKay is my maiden name."

"She is Eleanor Hinchcomb," Marcus said from behind me.

The kilted man frowned, and I felt my heart nearly jump out of my chest.

"What does it say about any other names, Duncan?" He tossed this over his shoulder at the second, non-kilted man.

Duncan consulted a pile of papers. "Hinchcomb is listed here, sir."

"Then you're the one." Kilted frowned at me.

Apparently being *The One* wasn't what he'd been expecting.

"The one what?" For once, I was glad Marcus was speaking for me.

Kilted drew himself up. "Ma'am, I am Iain Alastair Donal MacIain, head of Clan MacIain."

"I didn't think there was a Clan MacIain any longer," I said, before I could help myself.

I ignored the accusatory glance Marcus sent my direction. My knowledge on this, as with anything Scottish, was an unspoken forbidden thing in our home.

But really. As if I wouldn't look it up. Of course I had. I'd told the police that the people around me called my kidnapper MacDonald. I couldn't remember if I'd mentioned the MacIains, but they'd been part of the clan. A...a sept? I think that's what it was. They were part of the MacDonalds. There'd been only a few, from Roderick's mother's side, when my thoughts were interrupted.

"We are still here," Iain MacIain said in clipped tones, every inch of him radiating offense.

I sighed. I did a lot of that lately. "Sit down, Mr. MacIain, and tell me what this is all about." I sat down in one of the chairs, and gestured across from me in invitation. I didn't have the energy to fight with a stranger. I did enough fighting in my own home, thank you.

Iain MacIain remained standing, and the second man moved forward, carrying a large case.

"You are Eleanor MacKay, and also have the name Hinchcomb, which we have listed here, so this is for you. I am Duncan McAllister, and I represent Lloyd's of London." He held the case out to me.

"Why would Lloyd's of London have anything for me?" I asked as I reached up for it. At the same time, Marcus stepped in between us.

Iain MacIain moved then. "It is for Eleanor only." His hands rose as if to block Marcus.

"That's my wife." Marcus glared at him.

"Marcus, please," I held up a hand, meeting his angry eyes. Now he became a stickler about us being married? Where was that attitude when he was busy with his daily phone calls? To the *her* who was, apparently, helping him get over his dead wife before I so inconveniently returned.

The man neatly sidestepped Marcus, and gently laid the case in my lap, then moved back.

I looked down at it. It was a canvas case, like a messenger bag I saw my kids using. I stared for a moment, wondering what the hell I'd open when I looked in it. I didn't even know if I wanted to look in it.

Then I realized everyone was looking at me.

"You want me to open it now?"

"We've been entrusted with this for over three hundred years, ma'am," Iain sounded as though his manners were experiencing great strain. "It's been a sacred trust. I admit to great curiosity."

I glanced at the other man, who nodded, a half-smile on his face. "He's right, ma'am. This has been handed down for many generations."

"Well, okay. I'd hate to keep you in suspense any longer."

With the kids looking over my shoulders, I lifted the flap on the bag, and reached in. I pulled out a large wooden box.

Oh, God. I ran my hand over the carving on the front, feeling faint.

I knew this eagle. Without even having to look, I knew the words my fingers caressed. *'In Hope I Byde'*

I took a number of deep breaths. I will not fall over. I will not fall out of this chair. I let my fingers feel along the front. If it was there—

It was there. I leaned back, feeling as though the air had been stolen from me.

"I do believe that you need the appropriate key to open the lock, in addition to all the sealing wax," Duncan said. "The only thing we were to deliver was the box itself. There was no key."

He was right.

"Excuse me for a moment," I said. I got up, setting the box in my chair. I hurried to my room, and went to my jewelry box. I knew where it was. When Roderick had married me, he'd given me a ring. He wore one like it, and told me it was a key to more than just marriage. It was only after we'd married that I realized what he'd meant.

When I'd met Mara in that field, I'd been wearing the ring. I had taken it off and hidden it by the time Marcus got to Scotland but I still had it. It reminded me that what I had experienced, all that I had gone through, was real.

Clutching the ring, I returned to the living room. "I believe you are correct, Mr. McAllister," I said. "I think I might have the key."

How was I going to explain this? I'd told no one about the ring, not even Marcus. I could feel the heat of his angry gaze without even having to look at him. The thought of the fight we would have later made my palms sweat. I reached down to pick up the box once more, noting how heavy it was, and sat down, resting it in my lap.

"Mom?" Constance leaned down to put her arms around me. "Are you all right?"

I kept hold of the box with one hand and reached up to pat her arm with the other, the ring half on my finger. "No, but I will be. What is this?" I glared at the two men. How had they gotten the box?

Iain MacIain shrugged. "I do not know. The trust of this came to me when my father passed on. With instructions. Once I read them, I knew I'd be the one to deliver it. It offered this month, in this year, as to when I would need to carry out the delivery. I've no idea why the time was detailed so. But as to what it is, I hope that you are able to tell us. The instructions were clear that no one was to open it, and the bank had instructions that no one was to touch it until now, not even the head of the family."

I finally looked down.

It was the box. The lock confirmed it, but it was the box, with the eagle crest on it. I ran my fingers along what had to be very old sealing wax. The wax had darkened to nearly black.

Everyone was staring at me, waiting. I hesitated. Once I opened this, my life would be even more changed than it was now. I knew that without having to see what was in the box.

"Come on, Mom! This is awesome!" Dean reached over me to run his hand across the top of the box.

I resisted the urge to slap his hand away.

"I don't know that I want to, gentlemen."

"Eleanor," Marcus began.

It was not the tone of a loving, or even tolerant, spouse.

God. I could hear the lecture. When had we learned to speak to each other this way?

"All right. All right! Give me a moment…and I'll need a knife."

A sharp click in front of me and Iain MacIain knelt down, offering me a knife. My vision stumbled, if such a thing is possible.

He looked like…stop it! Stop it!

With a trembling hand, I took the knife, and ran it around the wax seal on the box. It crumbled easily into my lap. I handed the knife back and let my hands rest on top of the eagle.

On the badge of Clan MacIain. Roderick told me about this—from his mother, who was a MacIain. She brought the box and the rings with her to marriage. A family tradition on her side, Roderick had said.

I inhaled deeply, dragging the air to my toes. I needed it. I fit the face of the ring into the lock, and turned. The room was so quiet I'm sure everyone heard the soft *click*, and then I opened the lid.

The fragrance I remembered. I'd smelled it just over two weeks ago when the women had harvested it. The wonderful smell of lavender wafted out in front of me, obscuring everything and everyone in my front room. When I'd left, it had not yet dried.

Instead, I saw a darkened hall with a huge fire at either end, and I sat in the middle, my stool close to the chair of the laird. I took care not to meet the eyes of many around me, not wanting to see the varying expressions. The fires had herbs sprinkled in them, and tonight it was lavender.

I closed my eyes. When had he done this? I could smell the lavender as clearly as when I'd been there. As though this was lavender I myself had helped to gather. The thought made me weak.

"Mom, there's a letter!" Dean's voice in my ear.

I slowly opened my eyes and reached in the box, taking out the letter.

Turning it over, I ran my fingers across the seal. I knew it well.

His voice, coming at me from the grave. What the hell?

I could feel the sweat forming under my arms and neck as I broke the seal and began to read.

My Dearest Elenor,

I am sure it will surprise you to hear me address you thus given the past months you have spent with me, but you are indeed dear. You have brightened the last days of an evil old man, and I thank you for it now, even if I could not do so then.

I shall entrust this to my lawyer, my family being what they are. He will take this to an English bank, and from there, it should make its way to you, in your place in the colonies. Not only your place, but your time. I hope that this missive finds you well, and that your final journey took you to the life I kept you from.

I must offer you an apology, Elenor. When you screamed at me that morning, after I'd told you that you could trust me with your truth, I spurned it and you, and sent you from me in a rage. I pen this now, along with the instruction that will hopefully bring this to you in the future. In doing so, I can only hope that I might save myself some time in Purgatory. Please forgive me my actions. I could not see your pain for my own.

When I found you, when I came upon you lying senseless near the stones outside of Kilchoan, I was struck with a lust that I could not overcome. Having seen you, I could not leave you, nor let you go. To hear you tell me you wished to leave me that morning struck me in the heart in a manner I never thought I'd feel. I'd been hearing the senti-ment from you daily, but that last morning was different. You were telling me your truth.

All along, I could not bear to let you go. I burned for you, Elenor, as a man does a woman, but I couldn't bear to force you. I may be a sinner, damned to hell, but I will not have that on my conscience. While we never became Man and Wife true, I felt you my own dear Wife.

It is only when I realized that I would soon die that God spoke to me and told me I needed to let you go. It was then I asked for your truth on that morning. Once you told me, I found that I was weak and a coward, and I could not do as I ought. I retreated into anger and disbelief. I saw your face as I shouted at you. I failed in the task that God gave me. For that, I am truly sorry, my dear girl.

It has been a fortnight since you have disappeared. My men still scour the countryside, but I know your truth, and I know wherest you have gone. I shall never see you again, because the place you told me you came from was your truth. Knowing so, I can safely unburden myself without being unmanly.

After you ran from me, and it began to grow dark and you did not return, I thought on all you told me. I shrank with shame at my words to you. As the days have gone on, and you have not been found, I know that somehow, you've returned from whence you'd came. I do not know how, but I know in my heart that you have managed to return to where you belong.

Then I began to think on that return. How it would be for you to return to your place? Being nearly a year gone, your man would have moved on. How would you live? What had I doomed you to? A woman with no man to care for her lives poorly. I've seen too many women suffer after the loss of their man.

I determined that I would attempt to right my wrong. For I wronged you, dear Elenor. But I could not give you up, and as much as I could, I loved you well. And you, you have been good to me. Better than I deserved. While it seems impossible to believe, what else could it be but the truth you spoke? Given that, I have been fortunate in how you chose to behave with me.

Take what I send to you through time, dearest girl. Use it well. Perhaps it will allow for you to make your life yours once more.

Pray for me. Pray that I have not left it too late. If it be so, perhaps I will see you once I have served my deserv'd time in Purgatory.

Your Loving Husband & Obedient Serv't,

Roderick Iain Rupert McEan MacDonald

The letter fluttered from my hands, and I fell back into the chair, overcome.

CHAPTER 6

I couldn't open my eyes, nor did I really want to. Around me, it was as though chickens were clucking in a frenzy. I could hear the noise, and scuffling, and arguing...that wasn't chickens.

Slowly, I came back to the world, but I kept my eyes closed. It seemed safer for the moment.

"What the hell do you think you're doing, coming here and upsetting my wife? She's recovering from...from a kidnapping!" Marcus yelled.

"I do not wish to upset your wife, sir," came the rumbling growl of Iain MacIain. So like his grumbly ancestor, Roderick. "I am merely fulfilling a long-standing duty as head of my clan. I've no wish to upset anyone. If we could see what else is in the box, it long being a wonder to the family, we will be on our way."

"If the box belongs to Ellie, then that's all you need to know. You've delivered it." Marcus sounded mulish, and, I hated to admit, a little childish. What had happened to Marcus in the past year? Had I put that tone there? I felt more for him in that moment than I had since I'd returned. Then I remembered *her*, and I let the moment pass.

"Mom's waking up," Constance's voice broke in between the two men. "Mom, are you okay?"

I shook my head, and rubbed my eyes with one hand, keeping the other on the box. "I don't know what I am, sweetie."

"Can we see what's in the bag?" Dean nearly hopped in excitement.

I peered into the box. It was a bag, a sporran. Roderick had many. This was an old one, the fur from the badger head flap worn and glossy. I'd seen him wear this when he worked among his crofters, knowing he'd get covered in muck. I smiled. Thrifty to the end. Not knowing if this would ever get to me, he wouldn't use his best, or even second best, sporran.

I lifted it out and almost couldn't. What the hell was in here?

I opened the flap.

"Eww, what is that?" Constance backed up.

"A badger head. Popular at the time," I answered absently.

Reaching in, my hand didn't get far.

"Marcus? Can you take the box? And Dean? Find the letter, please. I don't want to lose it."

Marcus took the box, and I could feel the weight of… oh, of all sorts of shit coming off him. It was like a thundercloud. Oh, well. He'd have to wait.

Dean reached down under the chair. "Got it, Mom!" He handed it to me.

I folded it along the creases carefully. I wanted no one reading it but me. I could already tell that would be a difficult feat. But I would manage it. This letter was mine. Mine alone.

"Thanks, sweetie," I tucked it into my lap. "It's old. I don't want it ruined."

I turned over the sporran, and gold coins fell out into my lap.

"Whoa," the kids said in unison.

"Where the hell did he get all these guineas?" I muttered.

"Are those real?" Marcus asked.

Iain and Duncan didn't say anything.

I shook the pouch, and something small fell onto the gleaming pile of gold.

A ring.

Fingers shaking again, I picked up the ring.

It was small and gold. A double heart shaped ruby sat in the center, with brilliants on either side of it. A gold crown topped the center stone.

"A luckenbooth," I whispered. *His* luckenbooth. I fumbled, dropping the ring. The one that matched the ring I'd used to open the lock.

"What?" Constance asked.

"It's called a luckenbooth," I said. I didn't know if she heard me.

A ring exchanged between couples at the time of marriage. Roderick had shaken the ring in my face, telling me I should be proud to wear it—I looked up to see all the faces looking down at me.

"Ma'am, why did Roderick MacDonald leave this to you?" Iain bent down, reaching to pick up the ring.

I snatched it away from his hand. "I don't know."

"Don't you?" He looked at me intently.

"It doesn't matter. This is Ellie's, so thank you for delivering it," Marcus stood up from where he'd been leaning over me, and took a few steps towards the door.

Iain MacIain looked very much like he wanted to say

something, a lot of somethings, in fact. Duncan put his hand on Iain's arm.

"Ms. Eleanor, if you would, I will need your signature that you are the Eleanor MacKay Hinchcomb this has been intended for. Then we will be happy to leave you to your family."

Nodding, not really sure what I was agreeing to, I took the pen he offered, and shakily signed my name. Duncan looked over the paperwork, and gave a satisfied nod. Then he looked up at me, and smiled.

"That takes care of it, ma'am. Thank you for being patient with us. It's not often a three-hundred year old mystery gets solved in front of you." He looked longingly at my middle, and I was nearly offended until I realized he really, *really* wanted to read the letter which still lay in my lap.

Along with everyone else in the room.

No. No one else would ever read that. That was mine, payment for the past year. I felt the weight of the gold coins in my lap.

"Constance, would you see these gentlemen out?" I smiled up at my daughter. "I seem to be rather stuck," I gestured at the coins and gave a little laugh. I hoped I didn't sound as insane as I felt.

She came out from behind me, and walked to the door. Marcus came to stand next to me, placing a proprietary hand on my shoulder. I resisted the urge to brush it off.

I could tell that Duncan tugged at Iain's arm. Iain shrugged him off, and stepped closer to me. Marcus' hand tightened on me.

"Ms. Eleanor, should you have any further questions, please feel free to contact me. While our records are not the best, we'll answer anything we can." He reached into his pocket and drew out a card, handing it over to me.

I saw Marcus reaching for it, and I thrust my hand out, taking the card before Marcus could.

"Thank you, Mr. MacIain. Should I need answers about this, I will be sure to ask."

He bowed, and turned abruptly. Duncan gave a smaller bow, and the two of them walked out the front door.

Leaving havoc in their wake.

"I don't know, Marcus! What do you want me to tell you?" I threw up my hands. This discussion had become an argument. We both did our best to temper our voices, so as to not alert the kids.

I'd tucked the gold back into the sporran, and then I put it and the letter back into the box. I'd been carrying the box around with me ever since. I couldn't seem to let it go.

"How about the truth, Ellie? First, you disappear for nearly a year. Then you pop up, like a daisy in the spring, and tell me, Oh, hello Marcus, sorry, I fell into a rock and I haven't been able to get back. Then two assholes show up and prance around my living room, and you end up with a pile of gold in your lap and a letter you won't show me! Not to mention that you don't seem to be all that shocked or surprised by any of this," he gestured toward the box.

I glared. He returned it.

Then he turned away from me, trying to keep his anger at a reasonable level.

"Since you're still calling your girlfriend daily, I really don't think you have much to get all hot and bothered over in the jealousy department," I said mildly.

"I thought you were dead!" He yelled that one as he faced me again.

"Didn't take you long to get to that conclusion, did it?"

We both stopped. It was the thing we'd both been avoiding. I'd been gone for seven months. Marcus had begun seeing a woman named Deirdre three months ago. I had not wanted to toss this in his face, but it hurt. It hurt a lot.

Particularly as I'd tried to get back to him for most of those seven months, and when I was given the chance I didn't hesitate. Even though I admitted to myself by that time, I had rather confused feelings for him. I still didn't hesitate. I came home, expecting to at least find the life I'd left.

Instead, I learned that Marcus had buried me and moved on. Deirdre knew the kids. MY kids.

He flushed. "The investigators told me that you'd run off."

"Well you obviously didn't believe them. Having me declared dead suggests you thought something else."

"Well, you were with another guy!"

"Not by choice. I left the minute he let me go, Marcus."

"After spending almost a year sleeping with him!"

Apparently the moment of shame passed for him. I wasn't going to tell him that Roderick had never laid a hand on me. Not ever.

"You haven't given her up. I know you still see her. So stop with the overprotective husband bit. It just doesn't fly for me."

"What are you going to do with the gold?"

I blinked. "I don't know. I hadn't thought about it."

"I think we should sell it."

What? "We? This is mine, Marcus. It was given to me

for a specific purpose. If I decide to sell it, I will do so. But I haven't made any decision as of yet." I glared at him.

His eyes narrowed. "We're married, Ellie. Shared property. Or have you forgotten that?"

I might be off kilter tonight, but I could play this sleazy game as well. "Really? Are we still married? How can you still be married to a dead woman? You never really answered me when I asked for details on how I needed to address what you'd done. Because that's what you told our kids, Marcus! That something had happened to me, and I'd died, and we all had to go on and accept it. Four months, Marcus! That's all you gave me! While for seven months I lived in a smelly, dirty hell, trying to find a way to escape…" Tears filled my eyes and I whirled around, heading for our sitting room. I clutched the box to me. It hadn't truly been a hole, although the castle had been smelly. But I couldn't tell the truth. Not now.

"You did your best to make me a memory to my children," I said, my voice unsteady, my back still to him. I didn't want to burst into angry, noisy sobs. Not in front of Marcus. Not while having this discussion. "I will decide what to do with my gift, and I shall do it in my own time. Not one second beforehand." I found that the angrier I got, the more I slipped into the way I'd been speaking for nearly a year. More formal.

"Fine. Do whatever you want, Ellie. I'm done pretending."

I didn't turn around, not even when I heard our bedroom door slam.

CHAPTER 7

I didn't sleep much that night. Marcus slammed out of the house before the sun was fully up.

Since I couldn't sleep, I got up and began making breakfast. Pancakes, eggs, and bacon. Drawn in by the smell, the kids came in earlier than they normally got up.

"Where's Dad?" Constance looked around. "Did he go into work early?"

"I think so. He didn't say," I tried to sound casual.

"He's mad, isn't he?" Dean asked. "The whole Deirdre thing."

"Dean!" Constance admonished him. "Not our business, remember?"

"It's okay, guys. It's okay. I know that Dad thought I was dead, and he did what most people do, and got on with his life. I know you both like Deirdre. It's okay to like her. She sounds like a nice person."

Dean nodded. "She is, but she's not you."

"Well no one else can be your mother, Dean. But it's okay to like her. You don't have to pretend she doesn't exist." Damn you to hell too, Marcus. For doing this to my kids. Your kids.

"Are you and Dad going to get a divorce?" Constance seemed afraid to ask.

"I don't know. I know that things have changed. I don't know what happens from here." I shrugged. "Whatever happens, we both love you. Forever and ever. That will never change." I reached for them, needing to hug them. To reassure them that whatever happened between Marcus and I, there was a constant love for them.

Maybe a little for myself as well.

I thought about it after the kids had gone to school. I suppose it was a fair assumption that Marcus would think I was dead. I probably would've done the same. I might've waited longer, showed more decency—but you really can't say what you would do in that situation until you're in it. It didn't stop me from feeling like he had moved on with unseemly haste. Now that I was back, he wasn't happy about it. He already decided he wanted to move on with Deirdre, and he compartmentalized the feelings that he used to have for me.

The only thing was, he didn't know how to leave me, or push me out, without looking like a complete heel. Now that I had something he wanted, which was also something that would make his leaving easier, he was struggling even more.

If it didn't hurt so damn much, I'd laugh. Because watching him walk the tightrope he'd strung for himself was funny.

I thought about it some more. Did I want to stay with him? I hadn't told him everything that happened, everything that I went through. How could I? Besides, there was the small fact that I'd told people I'd suffered from amnesia.

The truth was, I was scared. When I'd finally been able to get back, it was because I got help coming back. I had thought long and hard about whether to tell the truth. I decided, with apparently some sense of foresight, that I would wait and see how things went. It was a wise decision on my part.

Marcus had been flabbergasted when I'd called him. And that was the overwhelming thing I'd felt from him when he'd come to Scotland. The lost wife returned—and he'd been delighted for, oh, the first five minutes I returned home. Couldn't look bad or show was he was really feeling in front of the police or anyone else.

I recalled Mara, who had stayed with me until he got there, giving him a very hard look more than once.

When I called, he was supposed to be away on a weekend with Deirdre. He'd informed me of that about ten minutes after the police left us on our own. To our supposedly happy reunion. He'd been planning to leave the kids by themselves—and while they were certainly old enough, something in my heart broke a little when he admitted that.

The kids at home alone. So eager to date, with his wife only seven months gone, he would leave our kids home alone. Something we'd never done.

At that point, I remembered thinking, what do I tell him? Will I ever tell the truth? Especially now, as we were strangers who were sharing the same last name and the house. In the spirit of complete honesty with myself at least, he wasn't even a stranger. He was the enemy. Or at least, I was his enemy. It was clear that was how he saw me.

The weight of pretending otherwise was nearly over-whelming.

I sighed, thinking of our shared history. I married

Marcus after college. I met him in college, and we dated other people, but we'd always been aware of one another. Then, as graduation approached, we decided to go out, see if there was something to the awareness. After that first date, neither of us could figure out why we'd waited so long. We were married within the year. Until I disappeared, everything been happy.

Or at least, so I thought. His haste in "moving on" suggested that perhaps I was wrong. But I'd never seen any signs of his unhappiness. Not that I'd been looking. Who looks for their spouse to be lying to them?

I shook my head, trying to convince myself even though I was all alone. How had things changed in only seven months? Ever since I'd returned, he'd been telling me that he felt we never truly connected, that we didn't relate. That he felt something with Deirdre he'd never felt before.

But he'd stopped short at saying he wanted to leave me. Now that I had gold that he wanted, I wondered if he'd ever be really honest.

I found that I was tired, and the thought of him leaving me was more shocking in that I'd never have thought this would happen to us. The mechanics of him actually leaving—I would be fine. I'd changed, in those seven months. And Marcus—well, Marcus was no longer the man I thought him to be. I remembered how I'd thought of him when I'd been gone. I'd missed him…but it wasn't the way I missed my kids.

I didn't know if that was more my fault than his. It didn't matter. Once he screwed up the courage, or Deirdre nagged at him enough, he would be gone, and the messy business of picking apart our lives would begin.

Honestly, it would be a relief. The last months of my life in the eighteenth century had been more than enough in the strained relationship department. If he couldn't be completely supportive, I didn't need Marcus or any of his mess. He wasn't really a man, anyway.

No, I'd seen what a real man was, even if I didn't want him for myself. And Marcus came up short in comparison. Roderick had been many things, some of them not all that great. But he'd been a man, an adult, and someone who did not shirk his responsibility. Even if he had kidnapped me.

After living with him for the time I was there, he'd done the best he could for me. Gave me the protection of his name, and his clan. Kept me safe from less honorable men. Didn't let me go, which was a mark against him. But he didn't keep me captive, either. When the chance came for me to return home, it was because I was out on a walk. Because he still allowed me as much freedom as he could. And after I'd left, he did his best to make things right.

Remembering all the comments his children made about me just wanting him for his money, his gift was even more poignant. How long had it taken him to hoard it?

I crossed myself, saying, "God rest his soul," and touched my lips with my fingers. Roderick—the name came with a pang—had been unkind at times, but never downright mean. Stubborn as a mule, and given to roaring when angry. But in the end, he showed me that he was a man. I didn't know what to think of it. I spent so long being angry at him. Deservedly so. But to see that right after I left, he changed — it made me want to look at the records that Iain MacIain had mentioned, and see what became of Roderick.

I had looked the clan up when I returned. It's how I knew about the MacDonald and MacIains of that area. Of Ardnamurchan. Named after the peninsula where Mingary was located. Briefly, because the pictures that

accompanied the sparse websites were hard to see.
According to history, they were a disappeared clan. They
did not exist any longer with any organization. Well,
perhaps not so, given Iain MacIain's irritation at my questions. But even when I was there, they were fading, disap-
pearing. Moving, marrying into other, stronger clans.
Roderick had been fighting a losing battle. To know that,
knowing how much I knew he cared for his people, hurt.

I had not found out much, other than he died some
time after I left. It made me both sad and glad. Sad for
him, and glad that I was long gone when it happened.

I got up again, and took the box with me. I'd slept with
it last night, refusing to answer any questions, or let anyone
—especially Marcus—see it. It was a talisman, like the
ring; proof that I hadn't fallen into some fantasy land of
middle-aged woman goes crazy. It was mine, and I had no
wish to share it.

Because of the time I spent with Clan MacIain, I was a
changed woman. My life now seemed one of desperate
luxury. In the seven months I'd been with the clan, I'd
worked hard, even as the wife of the laird. Women in that
time worked hard, even someone who had to learn everything all at once as I had. While I was forty-two, in that
time, I looked far younger than my contemporaries.
Roderick had been envied his young wife.

I looked at the box again.

I would need to take this to the bank. Marcus could
come home and try to take it from me. Anger made
everyone irrational. It would be better if I could get the
box out of the house before he came home. One less place
for his anger to land.

I'd told the kids the truth this morning — he left before
they got up. He was still angry from the night before. I
heard him moving around, talking on his phone although I

couldn't really hear what he was saying. But I knew he was talking to Deirdre.

Again, I wasn't sure I could blame him. I might, if I let myself get into a snit. Like me, Marcus had changed. He was different, too. It stood to reason he might want something different out of life when a new chapter presented itself.

So, enter dating. As far as I could tell, it was just the one. Deirdre, who was younger. And from what I heard from the kids, very attractive. Which led me to the thought of what was she doing with my husband, who was quite a bit older, and average looking? However, that was neither here nor there. Perhaps Marcus became someone quite different with her. Although how you squared his very short mourning period, his lack of attention to the fact his kids lost their mom, and his inability to tell me the truth about me being declared dead until I was home and stuck —well, shortly, he'd be Deirdre's problem.

Back to the box. I sighed. I went into the bedroom, and started to get ready.

After a shower, I thought about what to wear. I would need to go to a bank, a new bank, not the one I'd been at all these years as Mrs. Hinchcomb, and open up a safe deposit box.

Why was I so hesitant? I thought about it. It was because even though I was now back in my time, my head and my habits were still in the eighteenth century. It was going to these things—to anything, really—by myself. After I'd landed three hundred years in the past, I learned pretty quickly that I did nothing alone. Even as a married woman, I was never above suspicion. I spent a lot of time alone now, and it felt…off.

None of these musings helped me decide what to wear. All the clothing seems so light, so… revealing. I wasn't used to skirts that didn't swish around my ankles anymore. I wasn't used to not having several layers of heavy clothing. Even though the wool made me want to scratch my skin off at times, there was a protection, a comfort in all the clothing.

I finally decided on jeans and a heavy fisherman's sweater. I was comfortable, and I felt fully dressed as well. Both positives.

As I looked up banks in our area that we'd never used, I tamped down the feelings that were welling up. Why did I feel as though I were committing potential betrayal, all because I was choosing a different bank? Where Marcus was not known, or catered to in any way. Why could I not let him go as easily he seemed to let me go?

As I passed our bank, I kept on going and went to a local credit union that was well-known in the state. I went into the bank office and immediately asked for the managers. The young man approached me after I waited for a few moments.

"How can I help you?" He asked, smiling.

"I'd like to open an account and rent a safe deposit box," I returned his smile. I was nervous. I could feel my heart pounding, and I was sure my fluttering heartbeat in my neck stood out like a beacon.

The young man, whose name tag proclaimed him as Michael, smiled again. "Of course. We can help you with both of those things." He gestured towards his office, and I walked in.

Forty-five minutes later, I had a new account at the credit union funded with a check that I wrote from my account at the bank I shared with Marcus, and a safe deposit box where my past had been deposited and locked up tight.

It was hard to let go of the letter. I felt I wanted to keep it with me, so I could look at it when I needed to felt the need of... Reassurance? My sanity? The fact that it really happened? I didn't know. I didn't want to take the risk of anyone else getting hold of it. I kept the ring I'd been given at my wedding to Roderick. It could be the talisman that made sure I didn't forget I wasn't crazy, that all that had happened was real. I put his ring back into the box. It could stay there until I decided what to do with it all.

As I drove home, I thought about what to do for dinner, because that would be a good step towards... making things better? I didn't really know. But it would be nice to have dinner and pretend, anyway. I wondered what Marcus had planned.

Should I bother calling? Maybe I should.

I scrabbled in my purse and found my cell, which he'd finally reactivated. I called him at work.

Marcus answered with an impatient "Yes?"

"Hi, it's Eleanor. Leaving for dinner tonight?"

A silence, as though he were thinking. Then, "No. I need to work late." He spoke aggressively, as though we were expecting some sort of fight, or argument.

I offered none. "Okay. I'll let the kids know. I just wanted to see what I would need to make for dinner. Thanks. Have a great day." I hung up before he could say anything else. There was no need for any further discussion. After our words last night, and his behavior this morning, I found that I was happy he would be gone. "Working late." Uh-huh.

It didn't matter. We were better off without him. The kids didn't need to see his nasty attitude towards me.

When I got home, I found I was exhausted. Who would've known that the simple act of going to the bank and opening an account would be so draining? Even though I knew that wasn't exactly it, I lay down. I set my alarm, making sure that I would get up in time to grab the kids from school. Then I lay back, close my eyes and fell asleep.

I could hear the ringing of the church bells in the distance. Something was wrong. They never rang this time of the day.

I rolled over, scrabbling in the blankets beside me, panicked. "Roderick? Is something on fire?"

With my eyes open, I saw that I was back in my home here and now. Oh my God. I was dreaming about my life there. Why? I certainly didn't love him. Most of the time, I was mad as hell at him so why was I dreaming about him?

Did I miss the old bastard?

Everything else aside, even the fact that I finally started to fit in with the women of his household, I could never have gotten over the loss of my children. My children alone. I couldn't leave my children alone. That thought broke my heart over and over again while I was gone. It was what drove me to keep walking, keep searching and looking for the circle of light. My children mattered, and they would not go on alone, without me.

Interesting how Marcus hadn't figured into that like he ought to have.

But none of that explained why I dreamt of my life with Roderick.

I got up, and made sure that I was in the present before I went to get the kids from school. You never knew what sort of rumors had gone around about you. There was no need to give people anymore to choose from by looking crazy and rattled when I picked the kids up from school. They could take the bus as they'd been doing when I was gone, but I found I wanted to be there at the end of the day, be there as I hadn't been. The kids seemed happy that I did it. And because of that, I made sure that I looked decent every single day.

As I drove to school, I thought about how I was trying to merge the two lives that I knew. I thought about that I was going to have to find some way to settle this. I thought I had, but the appearance of Iain MacIain and the damn box showed me otherwise.

I had to find a balance, or I would truly go insane. Then, Marcus would be justified in tossing me over for Deirdre or whoever it was he wanted. I wasn't going to give him that satisfaction. Perhaps it was uncharitable, but that's what I was feeling right now.

I picked up the kids, and they were watchful when they realized Marcus wasn't at home. I noted that they didn't seem to expect him either. My anger at what he must be telling them, the burden he was putting on them, grew.

The next morning, he still wasn't home. I got the kids off to school and then went to sit on the couch, waiting for him. As the day stretched into the afternoon, I realized he had to be at work.

Getting up, I made a decision. I called him at the office and told him I'd like to have him come home. He sounded vastly annoyed, but I just didn't care. I told him very firmly to come home, and finally, he agreed.

I took the time to get myself ready, to tidy the house, to basically make everything presentable. I didn't even stop to think why was doing it. It just—it just felt better.

He slammed the door when he came in. It reminded me so much so Roderick when he was angry. I realize that perhaps Marcus had been a milder version of Roderick, and I just hadn't known it at the time. Only smaller, meaner. He didn't have the sense of responsibility to others that Roderick had.

Finally, he came into the living room where I was sitting.

"All right, Eleanor, what is this all about? I do need to work, you know."

No worry in his voice. No concern for why his wife, who had apparently suffered from amnesia for seven months, would want him home. No, just irritation. That his day, that his issues, that his personal concern and comfort were not catered to above all else.

"I asked you to come home because I think we need to talk. We can't go on like this, Marcus."

He took two steps backwards, and sat one of the chairs across from where I sat. Even though I'd lived in this home for years, I found that I missed the castle. Had I been there, I could have done this in the formal study, with a desk between Marcus and me. I couldn't believe I missed the castle.

Something I never thought I would say. Even if only to myself.

But I did miss it. The stones, the simplicity of it. Every-thing in my home now felt… Overdone. Too much. I took a breath, and continued.

"You are not happy, Marcus. You let me die. You put me to rest. And now, now that I'm back, it's just not the same, is it?" I kept my voice light, and put the hint of a smile my lips. I wanted him to be honest with me. I also felt slightly manipulative. But I knew there was no other way to get what I wanted.

"You were gone a long time," he said.

Had his voice always sound so whiny? Particularly as I really hadn't been gone all that long. I'd spent the entire seven months I was gone, trying to get back to him, and the children. I've never forgotten about him. I never assumed that it was a lost cause. But I held my tongue. I'd made my decision, and I knew that I needed to have him work with me, because he thought this was his idea. That this would benefit him.

"Yes, I guess I was. To both of us, apparently. I don't really know," I spread my hands wide, "As I seemed to have lost the time. I don't remember how long it was."

His eyes narrowed. "Well, obviously," he said with heavy sarcasm, "you didn't lose all that time. Because something happened. Otherwise, that MacIain guy wouldn't have shown up."

I shrugged. "I wish I knew what to tell you, Marcus. But I don't remember anything."

His eyes narrowed further. "What about the letter?" His words came out in almost a hiss.

He was angry. Amazing that he could get angry. Given he was still calling his girlfriend every single moment that he could. And the kids still saw her. Again, I need to let this one go. My marriage was over. When I'd decided to call him and insist he come home, I'd admitted that to myself. Having done so, I needed to let all my hurts and reasons for anger go. There would be time to mourn later. Right now, I needed to keep focus on the goal at hand.

"It made no sense, and..." I forced myself to look down. As though I were scared, or upset, or something other that was not positive. Something that gave him an upper hand. Then I looked up at him. "I didn't understand what it was about. And, it made me feel...uncomfortable."

"Where's the box? And the letter?" He snapped.

He didn't forget that, now did he? The letter seemed to bother him as much as anything else. I kept a smile on my face. I've been smart to take it to the safe deposit box.

"It's not here. I've taken it away. It doesn't matter, Marcus. The box and the letter are mine."

His hands gripped the sides of the chair. He leaned

forward, his face tight. "No, they're ours! You're not keeping that from me!"

I held up a hand. "I don't want to fight Marcus. It's very obvious to me that whatever we had prior to my disappearance is gone. I'm very sad, and I imagine I will mourn for what we've lost in time. But that's not the matter at hand right now, is it?" I looked at him, eyebrows raised slightly. I made sure to keep my face pleasant. Or at least, I hope it was pleasant.

In response, his lips tightened further. I didn't think they could, but he was very angry.

When he didn't reply, I continued. "You've moved on, and you're starting to build a different kind of life, the life that you want. Deirdre seems like a nice person, going by what the children say. If they are good with her, and she's good to them, I have no real objections to her. But I'm not going to continue on this way. I want a divorce."

"Oh, now that you've got some money, you're just going up and leave me?"

My mouth fell open. He was daring to ask this? When he was sleeping with someone else and planning a life with her? How I had never seen this side of my husband in the twenty years we'd been together? Maybe this was a blessing in disguise. I closed my mouth, and struggled to maintain my calm.

"Here is what I propose. We will file for divorce. You keep the house, and we will share the children. We'll make this as painless as possible and we'll go our separate ways. Then you can get on with the life that you are building."

"Oh, gonna keep it all for yourself?"

I kept my face calm. I was giving him everything but the stupid box, and this was how he saw it? What an ass. "If you want to fight over it, then we can fight. But you won't come out of this well. I was only gone for seven months. While that's a lifetime, in some aspects," I stopped when I saw his small nod, the tiniest of movements.

Somehow I didn't burst out laughing. He was really beyond the pale. Taking a breath, I continued, "While some may see seven months as a long time, as far as what's supposed to be a grieving spouse, it's not long at all. You took up with Deirdre only a few months after I disappeared. I hadn't even been considered dead yet. And you've never given her up, even after my miraculous return. There are plenty of records that will show that."

I stopped to smile as his nodding stopped, and he looked grim once more. "So I really don't think that you have any room to make any demands of me. I'll keep things as simple as possible as we work on getting through this, but if you fight me, I won't have a choice. If I must, I'll drag Deirdre into this."

This was my trump card. He loved—or thought he loved—Deirdre. He wouldn't want to do anything to bring negativity to her. She may equate it with him, and dump his sorry ass. I didn't know. I was just assigning snide motives. But it made sense. Who wanted to be with someone who brought nothing but misery into their life? He leaned back, and his arms relaxed against the chair. I made myself be quiet. Let him stew on this, let him push himself into it.

It was hard to be still. I felt like I was playing dirty. Because I was. But this was my life I was fighting for.

He stood up, brushing his hand on his pants. "I need to think about it. I need to get back to work."

I nodded. "Okay. Now there are things on the open, take your time." I looked out the window, refusing to make eye contact. Or even say goodbye.

For me, we were beyond that.

He didn't speak either, and a few moments later, I

heard the door slam as he went out, then the car drove away, and it seemed like he was giving it a little more gas than usual.

It might take a while, but I knew that I had already won. I knew that he would be giving me what I wanted. I knew that I would end up divorced, and happier.

My kids and I would be all right. Which was all that mattered.

CHAPTER 8

*T*wo months later

I looked around the little house. Once I'd given Marcus the ultimatum, he'd hemmed and hawed, and stomped around the house so much that the kids wanted to know what Daddy was so upset over.

I'd kept my temper, and my patience, and told them that Daddy was going through stress. My darling boy said, "Is that because you and Deirdre are here at the same time?"

I just looked at him. There was no nice or appropriate answer that I could give. I finally told him that could be part of it, but we needed to give Daddy some time, and space to get himself together.

Marcus did get himself together, and while he grumbled mightily, he agreed to my terms. I was right in my suspicions that he didn't want to drag Deirdre into anything she might object to.

After all, she thought she was dating a widower. One widowed a fairly short time, but a widower nonetheless. The appearance of a wife had to cause some challenges.

I grinned at the thought. Oh, well. Those were his challenges, not mine.

Now I was settled in the small cottage. I'd looked long and hard for a little place that would allow me to explore my affinity for the simpler look I'd grown accustomed to when I'd been gone. It had taken some time, but I'd found it.

The only problem was that it was a fair distance from my family home. But I made up for it by being available to take the children to school each morning. And I took them quite a bit after school, and on the weekends. It didn't hurt that Marcus wanted to spend more time "working things out" with Deirdre.

That made me laugh outright. While Roderick was no one's idea of a dream man, his mannerisms, and his method of dealing with the world must have made a mark on me, because Marcus no longer appealed to me. He was soft, and childish.

And petty. Oh so petty.

It didn't matter anymore. I was free, and for the first time in years, I had a wide-open future.

All I needed to do was to figure out what I wanted that future to look like.

I made a cup of tea, and sat down in my small living room, staring out the window. This cottage had a garden, and I enjoyed looking out even when it rained, as it did now. The rain beat softly on the roof, and I felt snug and warm in my little stone house.

Which is why I nearly fell out of my chair when there were three hard pounds on my door.

Oh, hell. The only person who got mad at me like that was Marcus. What in god's name could he want now?

I padded to the door, girding myself for whatever battle was coming.

I yanked it open, ready for whatever and saw—

Ian MacIain.

"Mr. MacIain, how can I help you?"

"Are you all right?" He asked.

I nodded. "I am. I was just having a cup of tea. Would you care to join me?"

He stared at me and I couldn't tell what he was thinking, but he nodded, and I stepped back to allow him in.

He followed me into the kitchen. "This is quite different from your previous home."

"It is, but it's more to my taste," I said.

"It reminds me of the cottages I grew up around," Iain said.

"Really? What a coincidence," I replied. "If I may ask," I handed him a cup, "How did you find me?"

"I went to your house—well, where you used to live, and another woman answered the door."

"Ah. That would be my husband's girlfriend."

"Yes, well, she gave me your address."

I led the way to the living room, and sat down, picking up my tea as I did so. Iain sat across from me on the loveseat.

"Is there something else I need to do? Something else to sign?" I asked after a moment of silence.

"No. I just—well, I was concerned. Your hus—your—"

"Ex," I supplied helpfully.

"Yes, well, he wasn't best pleased when we delivered the box to you, and I confess…I wanted to be sure that you were all right."

I laughed. All these men in my life so consumed with worry. "I am fine, Mr. MacIain. Although I thank you for checking up on me. I can't imagine that the last time we met was very comfortable for you, or your friend."

He smiled a little. He was a very handsome man, far

more so than his ancestor. Yet there was a great deal of Roderick in him, in spite of the difference that three hundred years makes in a family line. I could see it in his eyes that looked directly at you, and the set of his shoulders.

This was a man unafraid to face whatever that came at him. Yet his being here proved he was also a caring man who was unwilling to let suffering occur in front of him.

"No, it was not. I must tell you that I am glad to see that you have left, although I am sorry for your children. It can't be easy."

"It's not as horrible as you might think," I said, looking out the window.

We sat together quietly. I liked that. I didn't feel I needed to speak. Neither did he—or maybe he was too uncomfortable.

He broke the silence.

"Mrs. Hinchcomb—"

I held up a hand. "Call me Eleanor, please."

The smile was less forced this time. "OK. Eleanor, would you be willing to share what was in the box we left with you?"

I stared at him. Could I tell him?

"How much do you believe in things you can't prove, Mr. MacIain?"

"It's Iain, and I'm Scottish. We believe in a lot of things."

I got up. "Then let me fix us something to eat, and get more to drink, maybe something stronger. I have a story to tell you."

*T*wo hours later, the dinner I'd put together had been eaten, and I'd gotten out the rum, making us each a couple of drinks. Iain had listened quietly as I told him. I told him everything, not leaving out anything. It felt good to tell someone, even if it was someone I wouldn't see again.

Perhaps that was what made it easier.

I found that I cried during the telling.

As I finished, I asked, "What happened to Roderick?"

"Well, as you know, he had no direct heirs to take over, having only daughters and them married into new clans, so a nephew became the laird after he died. There was a great mystery about where some of his gold went, and it was whispered he went to join you. He died four months after you left. From what it sounds like, I think he had cancer."

That made the tears start again. In that time, it had to be painful, and he must have had it when he found me. He must have been in great pain, and hid it under his anger and his gruff exterior.

"May the Lord have mercy," I whispered as I crossed myself. I wasn't religious, but I found that the habits I'd picked up in the eighteenth century popped up in times of stress.

"I'm glad to know the truth of it," he said.

"You can't tell anyone else!" I was nervous that I might have told him too much.

"I won't, but I do have one request."

Oh, shit, here it comes. He wants the box back.

"And that is?"

"I would like to read the letter, if you wouldn't mind. I'd like to see what he said."

"That's…" I was surprised. "That can be arranged."

"You don't have it here?"

I shook my head. "No, but I can get it tomorrow, with a little notice," I said.

His shoulders relaxed. "I would appreciate that. One more thing."

"Yes?"

"Why did he leave you what he did?"

"You'll see when you read the letter."

"Oh, you're making me wait?" He actually sounded like he was teasing.

And there was something else in his words, in his eyes…

"Indeed I am," I said firmly. "Patience is a virtue."

"One I fail miserably at."

He was definitely teasing. I think he was even flirting.

"I thank you for your hospitality, but I must go," he said, standing. There was a look of regret in his eyes.

I walked him to the door, and as I opened it for him, he swooped down and kissed me on the lips. When he stepped back, he looked as surprised as I felt.

"I'm sorry, I don't know—"

I stopped him. "No need for apologies, Iain. I'm pleased you did it."

His eyebrows went up. "You are?"

"I am. Now, what time will you be here tomorrow so I can get the letter for you?"

We made plans to meet at one, and with a smile, he disappeared into the night.

I closed the door, leaning against it, hugging myself. But he'd be back tomorrow. I was very pleased at the thought of seeing him again.

I went to clean up dinner and was elbow deep in soap suds when someone knocked on my door. Smiling, I grabbed a dishtowel and dried my hands as I walked down the hallway to the door.

When I swung it open, I nearly fell over.

It wasn't Iain.

Instead, Mara stood there, with two people behind her who were dressed very…differently.

"Hello Eleanor. I'm glad to see you're home, and that you've left that little man you married," Mara said, walking in without waiting for an invitation. "When I last saw you, you told me that you would help me if ever you could, and now the time has come when I must ask for your help."

My mouth had fallen open when she started speaking, and it hadn't closed yet.

Mara stopped, waiting for me to say something, but I couldn't.

"Oh, good grief, Gram. You have the tact of a bulldozer," the woman behind Mara said. She stepped around Mara, holding out her hand to me.

She was stunning. Blond hair, half up, half down, and wearing a dress that was so lovely in shades of green that floated around her. She was also pregnant, very much so.

"I'm Iris, Mara's granddaughter with better manners," Iris said. "This is my husband, Brennan. We wanted to talk to you, and ask for your help with the portals. You remember the portal, right?"

I shook her hand as I shook my head. "I remember that thing—a portal?—all too well. I want nothing to do with them!"

"You don't really need to do anything with them," the man Brennan said. Like his wife, he was stunningly attractive.

I felt very self-conscious about my dishpan hands and my casual attire.

Brennan smiled at me, and my discomfort eased a bit. He said, "Let's close the door and discuss this, shall we?"

J puttered around the kitchen, glancing at the small stone shed in the backyard over and over, waiting to see if it would change in some way. Even though I knew it wouldn't. I couldn't help it, couldn't stop staring.

Mara, Iris, and Brennan had been here until late in the evening last night, explaining about the Fae Realm, and all that was happening there. It was almost too much to believe. Wars, and goblins, and trolls and dragons—but who was I to question? I'd spent seven months in 1707.

The portals were the doorways of light that the people in the Fae Realm used to travel. I'd fallen through one—I'd told them about the angry man who yelled at me in English and then another language, and that had made all of them frown.

They told me they weren't sure who that guy was, but that he was probably up to no good. Remembering how he'd behaved towards me, I could believe it.

They had also asked if they could place a portal in my backyard. In the shed. I'd said yes, not being sure that I could have said anything else.

I got their promise that only a few would use it, if ever. That it was a secret, kind of like a Plan B, a backup. They'd described the three other people who might show up, and then, after depositing the thing in my shed—something I still couldn't quite grasp—they'd left.

So I got up this morning, and went and got the letter.

I wouldn't think about portals again unless I had to. Right now, there were much better things to think about.

Like Iain MacIain, and how nice his lips felt on mine.

And how I had the entire world open to me, for the first time in what felt like forever.

It was going to be a great day.

AUTHOR'S NOTE

This story has been waiting to be told for some time. When I wrote it, and re-wrote it, I kept trying to figure out how Eleanor went back. More importantly, how did she go back in a way that worked with my other work. I don't like orphan stories. Once I got into the Realm series, I knew how she got back. I love that she was minding her own business when it happened.

Tricky things, these darn portals.

And I like the idea of a Plan B. You never know when you're going to need one, even in a story about the supernatural.

So there it is. I told you, there is a reason that Eleanor's story is a Realm story, and she's a good guardian for a portal, even though she doesn't know it yet.

I hope you enjoyed it!

Xoxo
    Lisa

EILOR'S TALE

A Realm Companion Tale
Tale #8

CHAPTER 1

My anger rose like a living flame to the surface as I watched the scene play out before me. I could see the cadre of guards milling around. In the center of it all were Jharak, Brennan, and that upstart, Drake. They were gathered around the body.

Jharak leaned in, and then I saw a spark of fire. I smiled. He must have touched the ring. I had to smile, or I would lose my temper. That was my ring, and no other hands ought to be touching it.

I had to let the ring go, however. There was no other way to insure my safety, to insure that the plans I'd been working on for so long had a chance to come to fruition. The only question remained, was how to get Aine to be a part of things once more.

Such a thought might have to be a fleeting hope. With Ailla gone, and even with that madman Cian gone—I was on my own. Niles had his directions, of course. But I didn't have a great deal of hope for him. Against the kings, even against Drake—he would not last long.

I hadn't told Niles my thoughts. He didn't want to hear

them. He was convinced it was merely a matter of ridding the castle of them, because they would come—and then we would resume our plans and affairs as though nothing untoward had occurred.

I am Eilor, the King of the Dragon Realm, I thought to myself. No one is more powerful than I. Added to that was my knowledge of magic, and how to use it with the power of the dragons behind me.

The thought of the dragons caused an even greater pang than did the loss of my ring. The ring was a magnificent piece, forged by fae and dragons after the end of the wars. Wars that the dragons had started. It was meant to bind a fae man to the Dragon Realm, so that he could become entwined with the Realm, and access its magic. It also insured that never again would a dragon so overcome a fae. I thought about the deaths I'd seen of fae at the hands of dragons.

Why would anyone turn away from harnessing that which the dragons had at their disposal?

I'd never felt anything like the bond I shared with the Dragon Realm. However, having put the ring on my decoy's dead body, I felt the loss of it. I'd always wondered where the ring fit in. Now I knew. You had to have the ring in order to feel the connection to the Realm itself. I knew now this because I felt its loss. Keenly.

I'd heard that the ring bound King and Realm together, but I hadn't really believed it. It couldn't have been that simple. I'd thought for years that it was in part due to me, to my skill. I'd been wrong. I'd taken the connection and the power for granted for so long that the thought of not having it hadn't even occurred to me until I didn't have it anymore. Because I'd always assumed it was me.

It was not. That angered me as much as the loss. Then

I laughed at myself. No one liked to learn their own limitations, especially after holding a different belief for so long. Even I could be forced to learn that what I assumed was not true.

While I could see some humor in it, it was one more thing the damned Fae King had taken from me. Along with that son of his, the Goblin King.

They would pay. They would both pay.

Taking my Realm and all my power wasn't enough. They had to take my daughter as well.

I'd told her when she and Cian left for the small castle deep in the Dragon Realm to be careful. I'd sent Aine along with them because Ailla knew if she hurt Aine, I would be displeased. I felt that Aine might perhaps steady the pair of them merely by being there. Not that I would tell anyone that. But Aine had that sort of effect on others. She kept people in line, forced them to be more circumspect, less rash.

Unfortunately that had not been possible this time. I'd watched Cian over the past year. He was getting bolder and bolder with his family claims. He seemed to forget entirely in his quest for vengeance that what had allowed him to live all these years was the fact that he kept quiet, and didn't draw attention to himself.

After Brennan broke off with Ailla, it seemed that both of them decided to throw caution to the wind, and live out their plans.

Plans that could have never worked.

I tried telling Ailla this, once Brennan had spurned her and her plans with Drake fell through. But it had made no difference. She would not hear me. It saddened me that my own daughter, brought up by me, had so little sense. Aine was a far better daughter than Ailla when it came to thinking things through, being logical, and not letting emotion get the better of one.

Emotion was a sure path to death.

But back to Ailla—Cian was not worth her effort. He was certainly not worth her death. Because she'd thrown in with him, and stayed loyal to him to the end—far more loyal than he deserved—she had perished with him. I'd heard of Cian's last stand at the Fae Castle.

I sighed, watching the torches in the distance. Perhaps it was better that Ailla had died being true to what she felt in life. Ailla had loved Cian in a wild, untamed manner that heard nothing of sense, patience, or self-preservation. She'd excused him when he married Dhysara, and she no doubt made excuses to the end.

I'd heard that it was Dhysara who had delivered the killing spell. Who would have thought that quiet, calm woman had such passion within her? She'd loved Cian as well, so perhaps that had been the wellspring from which her strength came.

I shook my head, trying to clear it of the past. The past no longer mattered. Even the loss of my daughter, and the boy I'd raised nearly like a son, and Aine—I stopped. What mattered was what happened next.

I needed to plan. I kept emotion at bay, but like the loss of my ring, and my Realm, and my dragons, it hurt me to learn of the deaths of my daughter and Cian. While I never thought they would succeed in their plan to kill the entire royal family, I had also not thought that Jharak or Brennan would have the nerve to put them to death.

Ailla had told me that Brennan bore extreme guilt for what he'd done to Cian when they were children. Guilt didn't usually lead to the guilty party killing the offended party. But Cian was dead. So perhaps my assessment was not correct.

Which meant my plans needed to be even more careful, and more precise.

I had planned for them to find my body, and my ring—damn them—but after that, I wasn't sure. While I wanted badly to have access to Aine, she was no good to me without Fangorn. It would take anyone else other than me some time for them to find out how to reach the dragons, but Aine might do it. She was always the smartest of the three of the youngsters I'd helped to raise.

A fact which made her the target of Ailla and Cian even more than she already was. Everyone knew she was smarter. And it enraged Ailla.

Aine never fought back. Instead, she hid. I had no doubt that if I were to reappear without a solid plan in place, she would hide from me and all would be lost.

Therefore, I could no longer count on the use of her. Nor could I count on Fangorn. While I alone knew of the corridor that led down to the cavern of the dragons, it would be difficult for me to get in and out of the castle unseen. Whatever my plans were to be, they were hinged on everyone believing me dead.

It stung, though, to leave the fruit of my creation to the uses of others. Aine had been born after hundreds of years of failure, and she had recently met Fangorn. Things had been proceeding nicely, even though Fangorn roared at me the last time I'd seen him.

"I will no longer participate in your disgusting schemes," he'd said. His voice was raised, and it rumbled through the cavern. I could sense some sort of awareness, a movement of minds, from the ten sleeping dragons. They, too, felt the force of Fangorn's anger. It made me envious, as it always did, of their ability to think and feel collectively. Even with my necklace, and the pendant I'd created,

I was not able to access the minds of the dragons like a dragon. I was a bystander.

"I have no idea what you mean," I said, keeping my head bent over my journal. I wanted to record how I'd noted the reaction of the other dragons. Was it just anger? Or extreme emotion?

"I know what you are planning. I will not do it. She is my daughter, the daughter of my son. There will be no more life from me, Eilor. No more," his voice dropped.

The sound rattled my bones. To cover my shock, I closed the book and forced myself to gaze mildly at him. I could feel the power radiating from Fangorn, and I wasn't even a dragon. I needed to remain calm, to not let him see that he'd affected me in any way.

"You will do as you are bid, or those you care for, those around you, shall suffer."

I locked gazes with him. His eyes glowed a fierce green, and had he been in dragon form, I might have worried that he planned to burn me. But as it was—

"Should you refuse anything I require, I will kill them, one by one," I gestured with my pen to either side of the cage where Fangorn resided, "And then I will kill Aine in front of you. You, however, shall remain." I smiled, and went back to my journal.

Fangorn had turned his back to me, moving as far away from the bars of the cage as he could get, and refused to have anything to do with me from that point on.

Had I not been trying to manage Ailla, I would have made him pay. I should have then, when I had the ability.

Now, I would not be able to.

But perhaps...I tapped my lip, thinking. A part of me watched as the two kings—perhaps a third, given Jharak's affection for his human-born son—had the decoy body removed and then opened portals. I didn't move until after the last of the light had died away.

Now everyone thought I was dead. It was time to use that to my advantage.

The first thing was to leave the Realm. The thought created an ache in my chest, but it had to be done.

The question was, where to go? I needed to hide and gather my resources.

CHAPTER 2

*I*n the end, I decided that the Human Realm would be the safest for me. None of the fae liked going to the Human Realm. They were backward savages, not familiar with magic, treating it as something to fear and destroy.

So no one would look for me.

I would need to be careful—the Watchers guarded the Veil, and I knew of the Captain. He was a veteran soldier, devoted to Jharak. If he were to catch me—

But he wouldn't.

Thankfully, I knew of portals that were fixed, that could be opened by anyone with the knowledge of their location. Once, many had known of them, but I'd taken care, in my Realm at least, to discourage portal travel to other Realms, and to insist that families create their own means of portal travel.

That way, general knowledge of fixed portals faded. All the better for me. It made it easier to get around without anyone really noticing.

I debated, going through where I wanted to go. While I

was seeking safety, and a place to hide, if I had to go to the Human Realm, I might as well—

The thought hit me with the force of a blow. I'd been so busy with managing all the aspects of my plans here that I'd forgotten. Of course. The boy.

When Aine was born, she was one of a pair. The woman who gave birth—a stronger human than I'd ever expected to see—had escaped.

The thought made the heat rise in my face. To this day, I had no idea how she'd managed it. I'd kept that bastard Lionel from her. But he'd gotten to her somehow.

I smiled. Lionel paid for his impertinence. So had Fangorn, I thought. I suspected that Fangorn had shared information with Lionel via that communication that all the dragons had. And Lionel acted, trying to get to his woman, and his children.

But he'd failed.

Just as everyone who went against me failed. It didn't matter if I had setbacks. Today, watching "me" be found by those weaklings who dared to call themselves kings was definitely a setback.

But I did not fail. Not ever. I would never fail, I never had.

I had no intentions of starting now.

So where would the human woman have taken the boy? I'd never thought she stayed in any of the Realms. Although I'd looked, I'd found no trace of her, or of the child. I cursed my hasty retreat from the Dragon Castle. I'd forgotten to bring my journal. It didn't matter in that no one would ever find them. But it was my record, and—

I shook my head. No matter. I knew all that was contained within my journal. It was mine. And I would use the information.

The woman. Where had I found them? I closed my eyes, thinking.

A place in the Human Realm…a large town. A city. When my scouts had found Lionel, it had been after a long period of time of following him. He was wary, and disappeared in the crowds of people.

I tried to see the small dwelling we'd seen them in. I'd joined my scouts, watching with them. I could ask the scouts, had I not killed them after they returned Lionel and his human to me.

And if everyone didn't think me dead.

This was merely a larger setback than I was used to. Not insurmountable. I sighed, closing my eyes. I could see the shabby place. Dirty, with trash and papers blowing into the yard. Paper held so little value for humans that they tossed it to the ground.

My eyes snapped open. There was an old, old portal nearby. I could use it. If I remembered correctly, it was not one that led to the city. But I could make it bend to my will.

I smiled, getting up, and brushing myself off.

As I walked, I focused on the picture in my mind. After all this time, the dwelling might be different, or even gone. It hadn't looked all that stable when I'd been there last. But it would get me to the place where I needed to be.

The woman—what had her name been? Maria. That's what it was. Maria. She was hurting. She was weak. I honestly didn't expect her to live when I brought her back, but I think the dragon blood of her children kept her alive. Once they were born, there was still a mingling of the blood.

I spit off to the side at the idea. Mingled blood. What was wrong with being fae? Unless, of course, you could be fae and dragon. That was a blood mix that had no negatives. The dragon magic was far more powerful than anyone suspected. I'd never told anyone, either. Certainly not Jharak.

It was a secret of the Dragon Realm, and I am the Dragon King. Dragons do not share. We keep what is ours.

I'd tried for years to get blood from Fangorn, but he was too wily, too aware. I could never catch him off guard. I'd nearly lost an arm the one time I came close. And even then, I'd only gotten the blood I used for my pendant by wiping of four drops of his blood from my face.

I smiled at the memory.

The cavern was dimly lit. I'd spelled the torches to stay low, so as not to alert Fangorn. Niles and I had been working on a magic that would extract a piece of scale and blood from the dragon. I'd gotten the idea from something I'd seen Lionel do, with a thin piece of metal he called a needle. He stuck it into himself, and it…well, I don't know what it did.

To this day, I still had no idea why he stuck himself with something that looked like a poorly made miniature sword. But he did, and he was pleased when he did so.

It put something into him. There was a container on top of the sword, the needle, and some kind of liquid was injected into him. I'd demanded to know what he was doing, and he laughed in my face, and said, "Sorry, Eilor. No more notes for your little book."

I'd slapped him, and taken the needle.

But after watching him, Niles and I wondered if it were possible to put some of Fangorn into a fae. Maybe we didn't need to keep breeding him with woman who were not up to the task. Maybe we could add some of Fangorn into a fae child.

I sighed, remembering. I'd been so close! Behind my eyes, I could still see it, as though it were happening now.

The lights were dim, and I crept carefully, muffling any noise I might have made with a spell of silence. I'd unbarred the door to Fangorn's cage, and continued in. I had my knife up, and a basic ready to catch his blood and any flesh I might capture.

I whispered the spell to bind him, and with a roar, he turned on me.

I dropped the bowl and leapt backward. I'd considered this might be necessary. I got out of the cage, and slammed the bars shut as he ran into them at full speed. Remembering how Lionel had pierced himself, I put the knife to the bars, and Fangorn, mad with rage, didn't see it.

The grazed him. I pushed it against him, so as to get through the dragon scales. He was so blind with anger, I don't believe he noticed. Then I yanked the knife away, and moved away from the bars.

His roar shook the walls of the cavern, and I watched, just out of reach, as he grabbed for me through the bars. The dust from the ceiling drifted down, calm in what was otherwise a storm of anger.

"You will never have a piece of me," he breathed.

I could tell that he wanted to shoot flames at me, but I'd barred him from it. He could not shoot fire until I released him.

I smiled. "I already do, Fangorn." I had Lionel, although he need never know that I also had just taken blood. There was blood on my face as well.

"Yet you want more," his anger filled the room, almost a creature itself.

"I shall always need more," I answered, and turned away. I couldn't let him see that my hands shook slightly. He'd nearly gotten free. Had he done so, even though he could not breathe fire on me, I have no doubt that I would be dead.

I was aware of that risk at all times with Fangorn. Hundreds of years in a cage, and he was still almost fast enough to get away from me.

Almost.

I smiled broadly, and left the cavern, hearing him muttering and pacing behind me. I'd let him be for a few days after that.

But I'd never been able to get that close again. And while I knew he sharpened his claws on the stone walls of his cage, I was never able to discover any trace of nails, or anything. Fangorn was careful and clever.

A worthy foe.

There were so few.

I stopped. I should be at the portal. Looking around, I saw that the rock markings were as I remembered. Now I needed to recall the spell that would allow me to change the direction of where this portal would take me. The fixed portals were fixed in both the Human and Fae Realms. But I'd discovered, through dragon lore, that they could be changed. It was one of the reasons the dragons nearly won in the war against the fae. They were able to shift the world to be what they needed.

As could I.

I sat, quieting my mind. I found that I was disturbed and unsettled. I suppose seeing your enemies triumph for the moment could be allowed to have such an effect.

I closed my eyes. The dwelling where we'd found Lionel was near a lot of larger, even cruder buildings. Would the woman and boy be there? I focused on what I remembered of Maria, and the essence of the boy.

If they were still alive.

It must be the events of the day that were allowing me to think in such a defeatist fashion.

After a time, I stood. My memories were as clear as

they were ever going to be. I needed to go, I needed to leave the Dragon Realm. I could no longer tarry here.

I opened the portal, focusing on what I would need to do to change the direction of it when a woman stumbled in from the Human Realm.

Humans were always where you didn't want them to be.

Her hair flew up around her head as she fell with a cry.

I rushed forward. "Stupid woman, get out of the way!" I pushed her as I shouted, and kicked her to get her out of the portal. She fell to the ground, on what side, I couldn't be sure.

I didn't care. I didn't have long and I certainly couldn't worry about her. "Take me to the boy of the dragon!" I shouted in the language of the dragons, and the portal opened wider, showing me a different scene than the one the woman had fallen through.

As I stepped closer, I saw that she was no longer there. Good. One less thing to worry about.

But where was I?

I peered through the portal, trying to ascertain if I had been able to find the right place, the right time.

"Where are you, son of the dragon?" I said, casting my senses out through the portal.

After a moment that felt an eternity, I felt…something. I couldn't be sure but…there it was again.

I'd done it! I found him! I moved closer, ready to step through the portal, when a cry—the cry of a woman distracted me and the dark building I'd been looking into disappeared, leaving me gazing into a field of green with —the woman!

She lay on the ground, unconscious.

I cursed, sounding no better than a man in the stables. Damn her! Why had her cry pulled me from the spell? I leaned down to get a better look at her, trying to see if she had any discernable magic.

Nothing. No magic at all. She was nothing more than human.

Frustrated, I kicked her. She moved with the force of my foot meeting her body, but she didn't make a sound. Perhaps she was dead.

What did it matter?

What did anything matter?

I'd lost the portal. I knew that I couldn't try to manipulate the portal again. It would be off balance for a while now. That was no good for me.

I would need to travel deeper into the Realm, find another of the fixed portals. All without being seen, or being caught.

With a sigh, I closed the portal and gathered up my things.

But I stopped. I'd felt something. Was it the dragon child? I thought so. His thoughts had the flavor of Fangorn, and Lionel, and even Aine.

I could be wrong, but I would need to find another portal to be sure.

Adjusting the small pack I carried so that it would be more comfortable, I began walking to the place where I knew I would find another portal. Hopefully, this time I could open it without any interference from humans.

It was no wonder no one wanted anything to do with humans. Stupid, bumbling, clumsy—the woman had ruined my best chance. Certainly the one that would be easiest for me.

I hoped she suffered when she woke. It's no less than she deserved.

I turned my mind from the problem I'd encountered to the sense I'd gotten. Could it be the boy after all this time?

I had to believe it. I, more than anyone else, knew what their minds felt like.

"I am coming, young one. And you will do my bidding," I smiled.

Thoughts of how to make sure he offered no resistance occupied me as I walked. Perhaps it was good that I had a walk of several days ahead of me. I would need it to plan.

Not only to find the boy, but to make sure that I could subdue him, and bring him back. Then, how would I use him to restore myself.

I laughed out loud. "Enjoy your respite," I said, thinking of all my enemies. "It will not be long!"

AUTHOR'S NOTE

This is the official end of The Realm Companion Tales. I love the crazy of Eilor. He is truly a madman, completely convinced of his own rightness. In his head, he deserves everything he wants. Plus even more!

Best kind of villain. He is disciplined and focused. I like this about him, in contrast to Cian, who…let's face it, struggled with keeping it all together.

Like all characters, Eilor wants something. He thinks he has a way to get it. And now, like a lot of people, he gets hyper-focused. His dedication is like, eight hundred years strong, so he's *really* focused, LOL.

But there's a reason that EILOR'S TALE is the last of The Realm Companion Tales. He's still out there, still on his mission. There's also a reason it's the shortest Tale. Eilor's ongoing mission takes us into the next series, coming in 2018.

Join me as we get to know THE DRAGON THIEF.

To keep up with all the newest releases, join my Reader's Group!

If you can't access the Reader's Group link, go to
www.lisamanifold.com/news

Xoxo
Lisa

ABOUT THE AUTHOR

Lisa Manifold is a *USA Today* Bestselling Author of fantasy, paranormal, and romance stories. She moved to Colorado as an adult and has no plans of living anywhere else. She is a consummate reader, often running late because "Just one more page!" She is a fan of all things Con, and has an entire room devoted to the costumes created for Cons. She serves on the board of Rocky Mountain Fiction Writers as the Independent Published Author Liaison, and in 2016, was named the RMFW Independent Writer of the Year.

Lisa is the author of the fae paranormal romance series The Realm, the Grimm fairy tale retelling Sisters of the Curse series, the Djinn Everlasting series which follows a free-lance djinn, the Aumahnee Prophecy urban fantasy series, and the urban fantasy series The Dragon Thief.

She lives as close to the mountains as possible with her husband, children, and four red, attentive rescue dogs.

Stay in touch!
Website: www.lisamanifold.com
Or one of the links below.

f facebook.com/authorlisamanifold

🐦 twitter.com/LMManifold

a amazon.com/Lisa-Manifold

BB bookbub.com/profile/lisa-manifold

g goodreads.com/LisaManifold

ALSO BY LISA MANIFOLD

Dragon Thief

Dragon Lost

Dragon Found (2018)

Dragon Revealed (2018)

Dragon Returned (2018)

Dragon Revealed (2018)

The Realm Series

Heart of the Goblin King

To Wed the Goblin King

Realms of the Goblin King

Rise of the Dragon King

The Companion Tales, Volume I

The Companion Tales, Volume II (2018)

The Aumahnee Prophecy

with Corinne O'Flynn

Eamonn's Tale

Marigold's Tale

Watchers of the Veil

Defenders of the Veil (2018)

Tales From The Veil

with Corinne O'Flynn

The Portal Keepers

The Gimcrackers

Djinn Everlasting

Three Wishes

Forgotten Wishes

Hidden Wishes

Sisters of the Curse

Thea's Tale

One Night at the Ball

Casimir's Journey

Do you like being in the loop? Sign up for Lisa's newsletter! Shenanigans, book recs, and the latest news abound!